TALES OF THE MENEHUNE

Tales of the MENEHUNE

Revised Edition

compiled by
Mary Kawena Pūku'i

retold by
Caroline Curtis

illustrated by
Robin Burningham

Kamehameha Schools Press
Honolulu

KAMEHAMEHA SCHOOLS

Inquiries should be addressed to:

Kamehameha Schools Press
1887 Makuakāne Street
Honolulu, Hawaiʻi 96817

The paper used in this publication
meets the minimum requirements of
American National Standard for Library Sciences—
Permanence of Paper for Printed Library Materials,
ANSI Z39.48-1992

Printed in the United States of America

ISBN 0-87336-010-9

15 14 13 12 11 10 09 08 07 06 05 04 03 02 01   (rev.) 10 9 8 7 6 5

FOREWORD

These legends have been selected with the thought that, in length and content, they are suitable to be told or read to young children as well as to be read by older ones. Some are very old legends, common to many Pacific islands, and others are of recent origin.

The *menehune* were the little people of Hawaiian tales. As they lived in the mountain forests and only came to the lowland at night, they were not often seen. Yet the Hawaiians could describe them. They were two or three feet tall, the stories said, thickset and hairy. Some of them were never heard to talk while others talked with deep, gruff voices. The Hawaiians said their talk sounded like the low growl of a dog, and their laughter could be heard far away. The *mū*, a banana-eating people, were a tribe of the *menehune*.

These little people worked at night. They worked together and in great numbers. In a single night they could accomplish mighty deeds such as building a road or *heiau* or walling in a fish pond. Once they even took a spring from its rocky bed and carried it, bundled in ti leaves, down to the lowland so that villagers might have its water for their taro patches. At cock-crow all work must stop for that was *menehune* law, and a job must be finished in a single night. Men still point to certain walls left unfinished when morning came too quickly.

The *menehune* ate bananas, *poi,* small fish, and shrimps. They liked to eat the whole of any food so that no part would be left as there might be if they feasted on large fish or pork. In little hollow places on the cliffs they planted bananas, taro, and sweet potatoes. On the cliffs of Kaua'i their trails are still pointed out. Sometimes Hawaiian men, spending a night in an upland forest, roasted bananas in hot coals. At such times the *menehune* had been known to steal close in the shadows and reach for the bananas with sharp-pointed poles.

The Hawaiians learned that a man who was unkind to a *menehune* would be punished by these little people, while one who showed them friendship might be rewarded by the work of many, many hands.

One sport the *menehune* loved was to build a little hill and then roll down its slope. Their shouts and laughter at such a time sounded over the whole island. Another favorite sport was jumping from a cliff into the sea. The little men would bring stones from the mountains until they had a large pile on the cliff. Then a good swimmer would throw a stone into the water and leap after it, trying to catch it as it sank.

Once, as they played this game, a shark attacked them. 'A'aka, one of the men, was almost caught. The *menehune* gathered in an excited group.

"Let us punish that shark," said one.

"Let us kill him!" said 'A'aka angrily.

"Yes, let us kill that man-eater, so that never again can he harm *menehune* or Hawaiian."

Soon the shark smelled food, swam after it, and found himself caught in a trap basket of beach-morning-glory vines. The shark was killed. But the *menehune* never again swam in that bay.

Once a boastful *menehune* told his companions he could catch the moon. They laughed at him, and he climbed a hill to make good his boast. But when the moon rode high in heaven he came down empty-handed. He was punished for his boastfulness by being turned to stone. Many stones are found which legends say were once disobedient *menehune* or bad Hawaiians who tried to harm the little people.

*From Rice in "Hawaiian Legends." Used by permission
of Bernice P. Bishop Museum.*

ACKNOWLEDGMENT

Once more we warmly thank those teachers and librarians whose interest and criticism have helped in preparing these legends for publication.

M. K. P. and C. C.

CONTENTS

TALES OF THE MENEHUNE

Laka's Canoe 3
The Feast of Pī 7
How the Menehune Saved Their Fish 10
A Helmet for Kū'ili 12

LEGENDS OF MĀUI

Slowing the Sun 19
Lifting the Sky 22
Māui's Fishing 24
The Secret of Fire-Making 26
How Birds Became Visible 33
Māui's Flying 34
The Battle of the Wailuku River 37

OTHER LEGENDS OF THE HAWAIIAN ISLANDS

Pele Came to Hawai'i 43
Fish From Far Kahiki 46
Why the Mullet Swim Around O'ahu 48

Hanakahi's Fishpond   52

Makua's Prayer   55

The Shark Guardian   59

The Tree With Silvery Leaves   64

Hi'iaka's Pā'ū   66

The Girl Who Lived With the Mo'o   67

Hōlua Manu   70

The Coconut Whistle   72

The Sweet Potato Thief   74

"Help Yourself"   78

The Punahou Spring   80

The Waters of Ha'o   84

The Springs of Ko'olau Loa   90

Water Without Source   93

The Sun's Imprisonment   96

"Stingy Kamaka"   98

How O'ahu Became One Island 100

The Flying Taro 101

Naughty 'Elepaio 105

The Cave of Mākālei 108

The Young Chief's Companions 111

How 'Umi Found His Father 113

Can You Keep a Secret? 119

Index 126

TALES OF THE MENEHUNE

LAKA'S CANOE

Laka stood among the great trees of the *koa* forest. "This is such a tree as my grandmother told me of," he thought. "It is straight and has grown strong fighting the mountain winds. Such a tree will make a strong canoe, one that can fight ocean waves." Then Laka prayed and went to work with his stone tool.

All day he worked. At last the great tree fell, and Laka went home, tired but satisfied. "Tomorrow I shall trim off the branches," he thought. "I shall cut the log to the right length for a canoe. Then I must shape it, but I have no skill in shaping a canoe."

When tomorrow came he could not find the log. "I should have marked the place," he thought. "Was it here or over there?" He wandered through the forest, but could not find the tree that he had cut. He cut down another and this time looked carefully to make sure of finding his log the next day.

But the next day there was no log! It seemed to Laka that he found the tree. The place was right, and there stood a tree just like the one he'd cut the day before. He rubbed his eyes. Was someone raising the tree that he cut down? He would try once more. So once again he cut down a tree, marked the place carefully, and went home to sleep.

The next day he returned at dawn. There stood the tree he had cut down! Someone had put it back in place, and not one mark of his stone tool was left upon its trunk. Laka stood looking, thinking, then returned to the village to talk with his grandmother.

Next day when he went to the forest he took a digging stick. Right by his chosen tree he dug a little ditch, then cut the tree so that it fell over the ditch. When he finished darkness had already reached the forest. Laka crawled under the branches of his fallen tree and hid in the ditch.

He had not waited long when he heard low, growling voices on every side. He caught some words about lifting up the tree. "Now! Take your places." He heard the command clearly. The *menehune* must be all about the tree ready to lift it!

Quickly Laka scrambled out. The *menehune* ran in fright, but Laka had caught two — the chief and another man. "I shall kill you!" he said angrily. "You raised the tree that I cut down and wasted all my work. You deserve to die!"

The *menehune* chief answered fearlessly, "What good will our death do you? Can you shape a canoe, O Laka? Can you haul it to the beach — you, all alone? Set us free, and we will do this for you. We *menehune* can shape a canoe and haul it to the ocean. Will you set us free?"

"Yes," answered Laka slowly, "but if you do all this for me, what shall I do for you? I have not much for gifts."

"Build a shed for your canoe," he was told. "Then prepare a feast for us."

"I will do that," Laka promised. "I shall go down at once. Tomorrow I shall build the shed and prepare the feast."

Next day he built a canoe shed close to the beach and thatched its roof with leaves of coconut. As he worked, he wondered. Was it true the little men could shape and hollow a canoe all in one night? And would they haul it down? Filled with this wondering Laka again took the mountain trail. He reached the spot in the forest where

his log had lain and could hardly believe what he saw. There, right where he had left the log, lay a canoe. It was all shaped and hollowed. Wonderful!

Laka hurried down to prepare the feast. He caught shrimps, cooked taro, and pounded *poi*. It was already growing dark when he spread *poi* and shrimps on a long food mat, then stumbled to his sleeping house. There he lay listening to a humming sound which came from the *koa* forest. "They are lifting my canoe," he thought.

As he listened the humming came again, louder and stronger, until the village was full of sound. Stillness followed, then a short hum as the canoe was put into its shed. For a time Laka heard the sound of tools as the canoe was smoothed, and side pieces and outrigger fastened on. Then came the growl of low voices while the *menehune* feasted on their shrimps and *poi*. Once more Laka heard humming as the little workers climbed the trail.

In the morning he found the canoe resting in its shed. As he walked about it admiring the work, neighbors came. "Laka!" they said. "We did not know you were such a good canoe maker."

"I'm not," the young man answered. "The *menehune* made this for me."

Told by M. K. Nākuina in the "Hawaiian Annual"

THE FEAST OF PĪ

A legend of Kaua'i

Ola, the chief, wanted to turn some of the water of the Waimea River, so that it could flood the taro land. "Let us dam the river," he told his men, "and build a wall to lead water to the taro patches."

The work was hard. Day after day the men were up at dawn carrying stones, chipping them and fitting them into the wall. They worked willingly for this taro patch would give food to all the village. Moreover, Ola paid the workers well. Each evening men took home fish, vegetable food, or *kapa* for their families.

But one man did little work. That one was Pī. Pī was kind and jolly, but lazy. He liked to spend his nights in feasting and his days in sleep. Since he did little work on the chief's wall he received little pay.

"Mother," said Pī's children, "all the other boys and girls have fish tonight. Give us our share." But Pī was sleeping and had brought no fish.

Another day the children said, "Our *kapa* clothes are ragged. Why can't each of us have a new *pā'ū* or *malo* as the other children have?" But the mother had no *kapa* for them.

"Oh Pī," she scolded, "why don't you do some work? Your children are hungry. They go with ragged clothes and cry for food. Others work on the wall and bring home food and *kapa* while you sleep. Oh Pī, work that your children may have life!"

Pī looked at his little ones with their tear-stained faces. "Yes, I shall get you food," he said. "My children shall have all that others have." But work in the hot sun, day after day, did not appeal to Pī. He wanted to do some great thing and earn a large reward! He made a plan.

Next morning he went to his upland taro patch at dawn. He dug all his taro, heated the *imu,* and left the taro to steam. He was hot and tired, but did not stop to rest. He took the mountain trail and, deep within the forest, found a *menehune* guard. "Tonight a feast will be made ready," he told the guard, "a feast for all the *menehune.* You will find it beside the wall the chief is having built."

The sleepy guard knew that Pī asked for help. "We will come," he promised.

Pī gathered a backload of ti leaves and cut a small *kukui* tree which he dragged down. He opened his *imu,* peeled the taro, and pounded *poi.* His arms and back were aching, but he worked till the taro was all pounded. Then he made the *poi* into small bundles and wrapped each one in a bit of ti leaf. These he tied firmly to the branches of his *kukui* tree. Evening had come, and the workmen had gone home. No one saw Pī plant his *kukui* tree beside the wall. He stood a moment admiring it in the moonlight. It seemed to be very full of nuts, but each nut was a bundle of delicious *poi.*

Pī heard a humming on the trail above. The *mene-hune* were coming, and he must hurry, for his feast was only half prepared. While Pī was catching shrimps the *menehune* were at work. Stones were passed from hand to hand all the way from the mountain quarry, while others of the little men chipped the stones that each might fit its place. Meanwhile skillful workers built the dam and the long wall which was to lead the water to the taro land.

Before the first faint streak of dawn this great work was finished. Pī's work was finished too, and from the shadows he watched his little friends enjoying *poi* and shrimps—all the *poi* and shrimps that they could eat. Then he heard the happy hum of their voices as they hurried back to the forest. Just before daylight Pī went home to sleep.

The chief and his men came to work and stood staring in surprise. "Finished!" they cried. Already water was flowing from the river and soaking the taro lands. The men examined the dam, they touched the wall of the water course, and wondered at the careful chipping and fitting of the stones. At last they turned to Ola. "*Menehune!*" they said. "In one night the *menehune* have finished this great work, O heavenly one!"

"Yes," Ola answered, "but why did they come? I do not know the *menehune*. Why should they come to work for me?"

The men looked at each other wondering. Suddenly someone shouted, "Pī! He has made friends of the *menehune*."

"Go," Ola told a servant, "and ask Pī. If this work was done at his request, Pī shall be rewarded."

The servant found Pī sleeping, but awakened him. "Yes," Pī answered sleepily, "I saw how hard the chief's men worked and asked the *menehune* to come down. I made a feast for them." That night Pī's children had new *kapa*, good fish, and other food.

A section of that *menehune* wall may be seen today near the Waimea River. Men still wonder at the rocks, chipped with stone tools and fitted together in one night.

Translated by Mary Kawena Pūku'i from a Hawaiian newspaper

HOW THE MENEHUNE SAVED THEIR FISH

A legend of Kaua'i

All night the *menehune* had been fishing. Before the first dim light of dawn they stood about their great pile of little fish. "We shall dry them tonight," they said. "Some we shall salt. We have food for many nights." Then they went to their homes in the forest to sleep.

But guards were left, and as these watched and listened through the day they heard strange sounds — whisperings and, now and then, the noise of a sliding stone! "Where do those sounds come from?" the guards asked each other. "Not from the beach! Not from the mountain slope!" They listened and still heard the sounds.

"I know!" said one. "There is a narrow tunnel down through the mountain. Someone is coming through that tunnel."

"Many are coming!" said another guard. "It is those evil spirits who live on the mountain top. They have seen our pile of fish and are coming to steal them. Quick! Rouse the others!"

Soon a group of little men had gathered, discussing the danger in low whispers. "I have a plan," the chief announced. "Let us tunnel into the mountain and take those spirits by surprise."

At once they went to work, chipping the rock. So many were the workers and so great their skill and speed that they tunneled far and reached the small passage through which the spirits crawled. As the evil spirits came through their narrow passage one by one, the *menehune* warriors fell upon them, killing all. The fish were saved and gave the *menehune* food for many nights.

As for the tunnel made by the little men, that is still to be seen at Hāʻena—a dry cave reaching far into the mountain.

Told by Rice in "The Friend"

11

A HELMET FOR KŪ'ILI

A legend of the Island of Hawai'i

A group of *menehune* sat in the edge of the forest looking down the slope of Mount Hualālai and talking together in gruff, growling tones. "Let us take the top off that hill down there," one of them said suddenly.

"Take the top off that hill?" the others exclaimed. "Why should we do that? Where should we put it?"

"On Kū'ili, the smaller hill down near the coast. See! The larger hilltop is shaped like a helmet. Wouldn't Kū'ili look fine wearing a helmet!"

Shouts of laughter filled the air. "A helmet!" each *menehune* cried. "A helmet for Kū'ili!"

The chief joined the group to hear why his men were laughing. "Your plan is good," he told them. "When the Hawaiian people see a helmet on Kū'ili they will be filled with wonder at our power. They will think the *menehune* as mighty as the gods."

The little men shouted again in joy. "The Hawaiians shall see our power! Let us begin at once."

As darkness fell the *menehune* gathered by the hundred around the hilltop, and soon their digging sticks raised a cloud of dust. The chief walked about to watch the work. "The hilltop is loose," he said. "Be ready—"

Just at that moment, from the forest above, sounded the crow of a cock. "Cock-crow! Morning!" shouted the little workers. Dropping their digging sticks they ran to their homes.

"But it isn't morning!" someone said, peeping out. "Look at the stars! Let us finish our work. If we leave now the digging must be done again tomorrow"

"We cannot work after cock-crow," said the chief. "That is our law. Away to your mats, *menehune.*"

The next night the digging sticks fairly flew. "Ready!" the chief shouted. "Only a few hours have passed. We can pry off the hilltop and take it to its new place on Kū'ili."

The *menehune* cried aloud with glee as they drove in their digging sticks. Suddenly the cock crowed, and the little men looked about in wonder.

"Run for the forest!" someone cried.

"It is midnight. We can finish!" another shouted, driving his digging stick more firmly in the ground.

"Away, *menehune!*" the chief commanded. "Cock- crow has sounded, and we must obey our law."

The *menehune* scampered up the mountain slope, then gathered in the forest to make plans. "That is an evil cock," they said. "It crows to spoil our work."

"Yes, let us kill it. It lives in the '*ōhi'a* forest over there."

"You speak well," said the chief. "Tonight I, with two warriors, will find that cock. Never again shall its crow spoil our work"

That night the three searched the '*ōhi'a* forest. All night they searched. Where was the cock? "Morning has almost come," whispered the chief. "I hear the song of the snails." At that moment, near and loud, sounded the cock's crow.

"There!" a warrior whispered. "On that rock above a cave!" The next moment the cock was dead.

Gaily the *menehune* made ready for the third night's work. This time they were sure they should succeed. A

14

helmet on Kūʻili would tell all men of their power. And then they'd feast for the cock was cooking in the *imu.*

The digging was begun once more while the chief walked about watching. "The hilltop is loose!" he shouted. "Drive your digging sticks well in. Now! All—"

Loud and clear the cock's crow sounded from the ʻōhiʻa forest. "We must obey," the chief said sadly.

Amid angry grumbling the *menehune* climbed the mountain. "Why didn't you kill both cocks?"

"We did not know that there were two!"

"Now all that digging to be done again!"

"Don't grumble, men!" shouted a cheerful voice. "At least we can feast. Remember the cock in the *imu!*"

Eagerly the earth was taken from the *imu,* the banana leaves were lifted, and the good smell of roasted cock was sniffed. Then a voice cried, "It isn't here! The imu's empty! *Auē! Auē!*"

The *menehune* crowded close, and stared into the empty *imu.* With angry growlings they went hungry to their homes. Never again did they try to put a helmet on Kūʻili.

But they never understood just what had happened. The great god Kāne had seen what they were doing, and guessed their plan. "The Hawaiians must not think the *menehune* as powerful as the gods," he said and commanded his sacred cock to stop their work. When he found the *menehune* had killed his cock he took it from the *imu,* poured over it the water of life, and set it once more in the ʻōhiʻa forest. There it crowed at midnight and put an end to the *menehune's* plan to set a helmet on Kūʻili.

Told by Eliza D. Maguire in "Paradise of the Pacific"
and used by permission

15

LEGENDS OF MĀUI

Māui was the hero of all Pacific islands visited by Polynesians. People loved the stories of his deeds because he was clever and because he had helped men in many ways. In every island group the stories say, "Māui lived here, in these islands." Some Hawaiian stories say that his home was on Maui, on Hawai'i, or O'ahu. Because people admired him they liked to think that he had once lived near their homes. Here are some stories of Māui-of-a-thousand-tricks.

SLOWING THE SUN

Māui was the inventor of the kite. At first he made and flew a small one, then ones that were larger and larger until he had the biggest one of all.

At dawn he hurried out to fly this great kite, but it was not easy to get such a large one into the air.

"O winds, winds of Waipi'o, come,

And fly my kite for me!"

Māui shouted. The winds came rushing and lifted the kite. Māui ran, paying out his string and shouting,

"O winds, winds of Hilo, come,

Come quickly, come with power."

At his call more winds came rushing. Higher and higher rose the kite. Oh, glorious sport!

Māui still ran. He had paid out the string to the very end, yet he still shouted,

"Winds, winds of the ocean come!

Come to the mountains, come!"

The kite was like a live thing struggling on the string. Never had Māui had such a good time!

Then he saw darkness creeping into the valley for the sun was already low in the west. "Oh, why does he hurry so fast across the sky?" thought Māui, as he pulled in his kite and rolled up the string. "I wish the sun would go more slowly." Sadly he started home.

He saw fishermen paddling swiftly toward the land. "They have not had time to fish," thought Māui, "They paddle to their fishing grounds, but already the sun has rushed across the sky, night is near, and the men must paddle home. Why does the sun travel so fast?"

He saw farmers returning from their fields. "They have not finished their work," he thought, "The sun hurries so fast across the sky there is not time enough to plant or weed."

As he neared his mother's house Māui heard her women chanting sadly. "What is it, O my mother?" Māui asked. "What is the matter?"

"It is no new thing," she told him.

> "The sun hurries each day across the sky.
> Then follows night, bringing the rain.
> We spread our *kapa* out.
> Before one side is dry, night comes
> And we must take it in.

O Māui," she added, "ask the sun to go more slowly."

"Yes," Māui answered in a determined voice, "I shall ask the sun." But he knew asking would do little good. He must make the sun go slowly.

For several days he watched. He saw how, each morning, the sun came through an opening in the crater of the great volcano, Haleakalā, and so up to the heavens. "That is the place," thought Māui. "There I shall meet the sun and force him to go slowly."

He got coconut fiber and twisted a strong lasso. Taking this lasso, his war club, and a bundle of food, he climbed the mountain. Up and up he climbed through the dark. When he reached the crater he waited in a cave.

At last he saw the sun's light and crouched ready to attack. As the sun climbed Haleakalā one of its long legs, or rays, came into the crater through the open place. Māui whirled his lasso and caught that leg. He

20

drew the lasso tight and smiled as he listened to the angry shouting of the sun. "Who's hurting me? Let go of my leg! Who are you? Where are you? Let go, I say!"

Then Māui shouted back, "It is I, Māui, and I shall not let go of your leg until you promise to go more slowly across the sky so there is time for work and play, my mother can dry her *kapa*, and I can fly my kite."

"I shall make no such promise!" the sun shouted. The long leg struggled to be free and now more legs appeared, entering the crater. Māui struck the one he held. He struck it with his war club and broke it off. Then he caught another leg with his lasso. "Promise!" he shouted.

"I shall never promise!"

More legs appeared each moment. One by one Māui caught and broke all the strongest ones.

"What is it that you want?" the sun asked, and his voice was weaker now.

"Promise to go more slowly so that Hina may dry her *kapa* in a day."

"I promise," the sun replied.

"Perhaps you will not keep your promise," Māui said.

"I have no choice," answered the sun. "You have broken all my strong legs. I must go slowly on my weak ones."

Māui saw that he had conquered, and made a bargain. The sun promised that for half the year he would go slowly. "The other half," Māui agreed, "you may hurry as you used to do."

So now in summer the days are long enough to dry *kapa*, fish, and work in the fields. In winter the days are short followed by long nights when men may rest, watch the stars, or talk and sing around the fire.

Told by Harriet Coan in "Hawai'i's Young People"

21

LIFTING THE SKY

Long ago the sky rested on the earth. Plants and bushes flattened their leaves and pushed and pushed, raising the sky a little. Still the world was dim and dark for the sun could not be seen. Still men must creep and crawl about.

"This is not good!" said Māui. He braced himself and pushed the sky up to the tree tops. "Now men can stand and walk about."

Still the world was dim and dark. "I'll push it higher," Māui cried. He braced himself and tossed the sky up to the mountain tops. There, that was better!

But still the world was dim and dark. "One more push is needed!" Māui said, and lifted with his mighty strength. He tossed the sky up where it is today. Now the sun could come bringing light and warmth.

Sometimes the clouds come low and rest upon the mountains. Rain pours down. But not for long, for the sky knows if it should press upon the earth as in the old days, Māui would come again. And he would toss it up so high it never could come back!

From "Māui, the Demi-god" by Westervelt

MĀUI'S FISHING

Māui-of-a-thousand-tricks was a name given the hero by people who admired him. But his brothers, who went fishing with him, did not like his tricks. "When Māui is with us we do the work and he pulls in the fish." That was what the brothers said to each other, and they left Māui at home.

One day Māui made a fishhook. It was carved from bone, and as he shaped it, Māui prayed. He prayed to the gods to make this a hook of mighty power.

Next morning he asked his brothers to let him go fishing with them. "No," they answered as they launched their canoe. Māui scrambled onto the stern, but the brothers pushed him off. "Swim ashore, tricky one," they said and paddled away.

That night when they returned Māui met them. "Did you catch many fish?" he asked.

"The sea is empty," they answered. "We caught nothing but a shark, and it is a kind not good for food."

"You should have taken me," said Māui.

"You could catch fish where there are no fish?" his brothers asked, laughing at him.

"Take me tomorrow and you shall see," Māui told them.

The next day they let him enter the canoe. The brothers fished, but caught nothing. As for Māui, he tied the hook of power to his line, but did not cast it in the ocean. "Why don't you fish?" the brothers asked. "You boasted that you could pull something from this empty sea. Why don't you do it?"

"Not here!" Māui replied. "Paddle farther out." The brothers did. At last they said, "This is our offshore fishing ground. Now let us see you fish."

"Paddle farther," Māui repeated.

"But this is far enough. This is our off-shore fishing ground, we tell you."

"If I am to catch fish you must paddle farther," Māui answered. The brothers did. They paddled so far from their island that they could no longer see the line of surf breaking on rocks and beaches.

"This is far enough," Māui said at last. "Now listen to my words. Turn the canoe and paddle back toward home. You will know when I have caught a fish, for you will feel its pull. Then dig your paddles into the sea with all your strength. Paddle toward home, and don't look back. Remember, don't turn to look back!"

The brothers headed the canoe toward home and paddled. They knew when Māui caught a fish. They knew by its mighty pull that seemed to be carrying them away from land. They dug their paddles into the water with all their strength.

Māui was playing his fish. As he struggled he panted to his brothers, "Paddle! Paddle! Don't look back!"

"What kind of a fish has Māui caught?" the brothers wondered. "What can it be that pulls so mightily?"

Filled with wonder, one turned to look. "Brothers!" he shouted. "It is land Māui has caught. He is pulling up islands!"

Everyone stopped paddling and turned to stare.

"See what you have done!" cried Māui angrily. "I was going to pull up a great land, but because you stopped paddling I have only these islands!"

And that, so the story says, is the way our Hawaiian Islands came above the ocean.

From "Māui, the Demi-god" by Westervelt

25

THE SECRET OF FIRE-MAKING

Very long ago the people of Hawai'i knew fire. Lava flowing down a mountainside set trees and plants aflame. After the flames died down men sometimes found roasted breadfruit or bananas. Cautiously they tasted. Oh, how good! After that they tried to get and keep the fire. Men found they could light a stick at the edge of a lava flow. From that stick they could light another and another and so carry the fire home. Then all the village could roast sweet potatoes or broil fish. Everyone might feast on cooked food. But next day the fire was dead. With no one to feed it, it went out while men were sleeping. And no one knew how to make fire, only to carry it from a lava flow.

One morning Māui and his brothers had gone fishing. They reached their fishing ground and dropped their lines, then looked about them. Sea and sky were touched with pink, and the land was a gray line rising into cloud. Against the pale gray of the cloud one of the brothers saw a tiny column of darker gray. "Smoke!" he exclaimed. "Look! Someone has fire."

The others stared. "Whose fire can it be?" they asked. "It is near our beach. Someone has brought fire from the fire pit and has not shared it with us."

"Let us return at once and cook our food," said one. "The bananas in our ripening pit are ready. Let us roast some."

But the oldest answered, "First we shall fish. In the cool of the morning the fish are hungry. See!" as he pulled up a red-gold beauty.

"Yes," all agreed, "first we shall fish, then paddle back to cook our fish and our bananas."

Soon they had enough fish and paddled home. "The smoke dies down," said one. "I hope the owner of the precious fire will not let it go out."

"When we reach the reef," Māui said, "I'll run to get the fire and bring some ripe bananas. You beach the canoe." The moment they reached shallow water Māui sprang out and ran.

The brothers beached the canoe, made offering to Kū'ula, god of fishing, in thanks for their good catch, and gathered wood for a fire. "Why doesn't Māui come?" they asked each other.

Then they saw him, walking slowly, empty-handed. "Māui, where's the fire?" they shouted.

"I thought men had that fire," Māui answered. "But it was 'alae birds, mud hens. They scurried away just as I reached the place. On the ground I found ashes, but no spark of fire. Do you know what else I found? The skins of roasted bananas! The mud hens have taken all the ripe bananas from our pit, cooked and eaten them."

The three brothers were angry. "We'll watch those mud hens!" they cried. "They won't get any more bananas!"

"Yes," Māui was thinking, "I too shall watch the mud hens. How do they get fire? Can a small bird carry a burning stick from the fire pit? Perhaps they know some secret way to make fire." Every day he watched, but saw no mud hens.

After some days the brothers again went for fish. Just as they reached their fishing ground Māui turned to look. "There it is again!" he exclaimed. "The smoke! Let us go back at once." They paddled fast, then Māui leaped from the canoe and ran with all his speed. He saw the mud hens scurry away. He saw where they had cooked bananas.

Again and again this happened. If the brothers stayed at home to watch, there was no fire. If they went out in the canoe, smoke rose in a tiny column. But, however fast they paddled, the fire was out before they could reach the place.

"And we never see the mud hens bringing fire," Māui thought. "They must make it somehow, and I shall learn their secret. Leave me behind tomorrow," he said aloud. "If they see you paddle out the mud hens will make their fire, and I shall watch them."

As the canoe was paddled out in the gray of the next morning, Māui crawled quietly through the reeds. He had almost reached the place where the birds had their fire, when he heard voices. The mud hens talked softly as they watched the canoe. "There go those brothers," one said. "Let us make our fire."

"Wait!" said another voice. "One, two, three. There are only three in the canoe. Perhaps the fourth has stayed behind to watch us. Today we shall not cook bananas."

The disappointed hero saw the birds scatter. "They are clever!" he thought. "I must outwit them." That night he said to his brothers, "You three go fishing as you did today, leaving me behind. This one shall take my place." The others watched as Māui picked up the tall gourd in which they kept their fishhooks. He wrapped it in old *kapa*, making *kapa* head and arms.

The brothers laughed. "Why take that thing?" they asked him.

"The mud hens will count," he answered. "In the dim light of dawn they'll think they see four fishermen. Then I shall learn their secret."

28

Next morning as the canoe paddled out Māui lay hidden. "There goes the canoe!" he heard a mud hen say. "One, two, three, four. The brothers have all gone fishing. Let us make our fire."

In the dim light the mud hens had thought the gourd a man as Māui hoped. But that early morning dimness made it hard for Māui himself to see. Peeping through the reeds he watched the birds bringing sticks. The leader was rubbing something. Was that a wisp of smoke that rose? Yes, surely there was smoke! What was the mud hen rubbing? He must get nearer.

Carefully he crawled through the reeds. A small stone rolled. The mud hens had sharp ears. "Someone is coming!" the leader cried. "It may be Māui, the Quick One." With wings and feet they beat out the fire, scattering the ashes. Then they scattered. But the leader waited a moment to be sure no sparks remained. That moment was enough for Māui. He caught and held her fast. "Wicked bird!" he shouted. "You know how to get fire and have kept the secret from man. How do you get it? Tell me or you die!"

"If I die you'll never learn the secret," the mud hen answered.

That was true. Māui began to hurt her a little — then a little more. "How do you get the fire?" he asked again.

"Do not tell!" called the other birds from the bushes where they were hiding. "Oh, do not tell the secret."

"I must tell," the leader answered. "The ti stalk hides the fire. Take a ti leaf, O Māui, and rub its stalk with the broken stick that I was using." There was laughter hidden in the bird's eyes. She thought that he would let her go.

But Māui held her firmly as he broke off a ti leaf. He held its stalk with his bare feet as he sat on the ground.

30

One hand was free for rubbing, while with the other Māui held the bird. He worked with all his might. He rubbed a groove in the ti stalk and squeezed out water. No fire came. "You have fooled me!" he said angrily to the mud hen. "I shall kill you."

"If you kill me you will never know the secret."

"That is true," said Māui. "Then I shall hurt you until you tell me in which plant fire is hidden."

"Oh, I will tell! It is in the taro stalk. Rub that stalk, and fire will come forth."

So Māui rubbed. He rubbed a groove in the taro stalk and squeezed out water, but no fire came. Turning quickly, he saw the laughter in the mud hen's eyes. "Where is the fire?" he shouted angrily.

"Oh, I will tell you," the bird answered. This time it was green wood she told Māui to use. Green wood has just been cut and is full of sap. So, for all his labor, Māui got only sap!

This time, in his anger, Māui was ready to kill the mud hen. "Oh, I will tell you truly," she cried in fright. "Take that piece of dry *hau* wood that I was using. There is a groove in it already. Rub with the hard stick. You will get powdered wood, then fire will come."

Māui held the piece of *hau* with his bare feet. He rubbed with all his might, back and forth, faster and faster. The groove was filled with powdered wood. Was that a spark?

No, the smoke was gone. Māui stopped for breath and looked angrily at the mud hen whom he still held. This time he saw no laughter in her eyes. "That is the way, Māui," she said. "Fire is in the *hau*, but you must rub fast and long to bring it out."

The hero rubbed again. Smoke rose. He saw sparks in the powdered wood. Faster and faster he worked! At

31

last his stick was blazing. With the blazing stick Māui made a red mark on the little mud hen's head. "By this mark," he said, "all men shall know that you mud hens knew the secret of the fire and kept it hidden. But at last you told. Now all shall know."

And all men knew, for Māui taught them the secret of fire-making. Now meat, fish, and vegetables could be roasted in the *imu*, or cooked over hot coals. When men were in the mountain forests snaring birds or shaping a canoe, they could make fire to warm themselves. No wonder Māui was the hero of Hawai'i *nei*.

From a translation by A. O. Forbes, in the
"Hawaiian Annual."

HOW BIRDS BECAME VISIBLE

Long ago birds were invisible. Men could hear the whir of their wings and listen to their songs, but the birds themselves no one could see — no one but Māui.

One day a visitor came from another island and challenged Māui to a boasting contest. A crowd gathered and listened with delight as each man boasted of his island — its mountains, waterfalls, and forests.

"I must win!" thought Māui, and aloud he said, "I'll prove to you that we have something here that you have never dreamed of." Secretly he called the birds. They lighted all about on trees and bushes and filled the air with song.

The boastful visitor was silent while the crowd listened in wonder. "Spirits!" they whispered.

At last, using his mighty power, Māui caused them all to see the little feathered singers. The boastful man exclaimed, "O Māui, you have won! In my island there is no such wonder."

Ever since that day birds may be seen as well as heard.

From "Māui, the Demi-god" by Westervelt

MĀUI'S FLYING

One day Māui came to Hina, his mother, with tears running down his cheeks. "Why do you weep?" she asked him.

"For my wife. That wicked chief, Pe'ape'a-the-eight-eyed, has stolen her."

"You are Māui, the Quick One. Could you not catch that evil chief?"

"I followed as swiftly as I could," Māui replied, "but Pe'ape'a flew with her to his own island. I cannot follow through the air. Oh, Mother, what shall I do?"

"Go to your grandfather. He is very wise."

Māui found his grandfather. "Pe'ape'a-the-eight-eyed has stolen my dear wife," he said.

"You are Māui, the Quick One?" the old man asked. "Yes."

"Then go at once and bring these things I ask for: 'ie'ie rootlets, such as are used in making baskets, ti leaves, and feathers like those in cloaks and helmets. Bring enough to fill my house and bring them quickly."

Māui did as the old man commanded. "Good!" his grandfather exclaimed. "Come back in three days' time. I shall be ready."

On the third day Māui returned. His grandfather had made a big bird. He had made it of 'ie'ie rootlets and covered it with leaves and feathers. "It is ready," the old man said. "Inside the bird you will find cords. With them you can flap its wings and make it fly. Also there is a bundle of food.

34

"Now listen carefully to all my words. Fly to the island of Pe'ape'a. You will see its people gathered on the beach. Pe'ape'a will be there and your wife. Fly out over the ocean. When you return people will see you. Listen to their shouts. If you hear Pe'ape'a say that you are his bird, all will be well. He will have you taken into his sleeping house, and you can save your wife."

Māui thanked his grandfather, got into the bird, pulled the cords to flap the wings, and flew. For two days and two nights he flew, then reached the island of Pe'ape'a. He saw people on the beach as his grandfather had foretold. He flew past them out over the ocean. He flew far dipping close to the waves, then soaring high. As he returned he heard shouts, "See that great bird!"

"Perhaps it is my bird," said Pe'ape'a. "If it lights on my sacred box the bird is mine." So Māui lighted on the sacred box, and Pe'ape'a told his servants to carry the box, with the bird on it, into the sleeping house. There Māui waited.

Through the eyes of the bird he watched as people came in and stretched out on piles of mats. They pulled *kapa* covers over them and closed their eyes in sleep. But Pe'ape'a had eight eyes! One of them closed, and after a time four more. But three eyes were open all night long.

Would they never close? Māui dared not get out of the bird while that wicked chief was watching. Morning would come. Everyone would waken. He might be found and killed! Māui sent a secret call to Hina, his powerful mother,

> "O Hina,
> Hold back the night.
> Let darkness rest upon the eyes of Pe'ape'a
> That I may save my wife."

35

Hina heard and left the darkness resting on that island. Slowly two more of the chief's eyes closed. Still Māui waited. Would the eighth eye never sleep?

At last it closed. Māui slipped out of the great bird, and cut off the head of Pe'ape'a, for Māui knew he was a very wicked chief. Then the hero roused his wife and helped her into the bird. Now the bird must fly away, so Māui tore a great hole in the roof before he too got in.

Away they flew through the opening. Winds beat upon the bird and rain fell, but Māui and his wife were safe inside.

The grandfather was watching as Māui stepped out of the bird. "Where is your wife?" he asked. "Did you not save her?"

"Yes. She is safe inside." And Māui lifted her out.

They thanked the grandfather, and then returned to Hina. There was great joy because Māui's wife was saved.

From "More Hawaiian Folk Tales" by Thrum

THE BATTLE OF THE WAILUKU RIVER

Hina, the mother of Māui, lived in a cave behind the falls of the Wailuku River on Hawai'i. There she and her women made *kapa*, chanting as they worked. Now Hina had an enemy, a giant lizard, or *mo'o*, whose name was Kuna Mo'o. He liked to trouble Hina. He rolled rocks and logs into the river above the falls, thinking their crash would hurt or frighten the women.

Instead he heard Hina's laughing call, "Aloha, O Kuna Mo'o! Your rocks and your logs make a fine drum to keep time to our chanting."

The great *mo'o* snapped his jaws in anger. "Their chanting shall end!" he promised as he climbed the mountain.

It was night when he returned, pushing a huge rock. All was quiet in the cave. The women slept and would not hear the noise that he must make. He rolled the great rock into the river below the falls to make a dam. The water could not flow past the rock. Kuna Mo'o watched it grow deeper and deeper until it began to flow back into the cave "They will all drown!" he chuckled. "They will drown as they sleep."

Then he heard a sharp cry, "Awake, Hina! Awake! The water rises in our cave."

A moment later he heard the voice of Hina, strong and clear, calling to her mighty son:

> "O Māui, fisher of islands,
> O Māui, slower of sun,

Listen!
It is Hina who calls,
Hina, your mother,
Shut in the cave in the night,
Made prisoner here by the *moʻo,*
While water pours into our cave.
Come quickly, O Māui my son.
Come in your swift canoe.
Come with your mighty war club
And save us from this Kuna Moʻo."

The *moʻo* chuckled again. "She calls for her son," he muttered, "But Māui is far away. He cannot hear her call."

Māui did hear, faintly, as in a dream. He sprang from sleep. Had someone called? He looked about the night sky and saw a small, bright, fleecy cloud above Hawaiʻi. "My mother's cloud!" he thought. "Hina is in trouble and calls for help." He leaped down the side of Mount Haleakalā with mighty strides. He sprang into his canoe and dug his paddle in the sea.

He reached Hilo. One look at the river told him what had happened. No water flowed. The river had been dammed, and Hina and her women were in danger.

Up the river Māui hurried. He reached the rock which stopped the water's flow. There was no time to move it. With his club Māui struck the bank and made a water-way around the rock.

Once more the river flowed toward the ocean, and Māui heard his mother and her women chanting his praise. But he did not stop to listen, for he heard also the sound of the *moʻo* above. The great lizard was fleeing to a hiding place. Māui followed. When he found the *moʻo,* he struck until the earth trembled. Kuna Moʻo

38

R. BURNINGHAM

rushed out, seeking another place to hide. Still Māui followed. Again and again the earth trembled with the blows of his mighty club.

The *mo'o* hid in a deep pool where Māui could not reach him. The hero poured red-hot lava into the pool and hurled in hot rocks. The water boiled, and Kuna Mo'o fled again, this time down stream. Above the falls he turned to fight. He sprang at Māui, snapping his jaws. Māui dodged and struck, and the *mo'o* tumbled over the falls.

As Māui leaped down the cliff he heard the women chanting prayers — prayers for his victory. He found Kuna Mo'o weak, but still snapping his ugly jaws. Again and again Māui struck until his enemy was dead.

The giant lizard still lies where he fell, a great rock in the Wailuku River. He is beaten by stones and logs and flooded by water just as he tried to beat Hina and drown her in the flood.

As for the deep pool above, though Māui no longer pours in red-hot lava, the waters of the "boiling pots" still bubble and boil as if remembering his mighty battle with Kuna Mo'o.

From "Māui, the Demi-god" by Westervelt

OTHER LEGENDS OF THE HAWAIIAN ISLANDS

PELE CAME TO HAWAIʻI

Long ago Pele lived with her family on an island of Far Kahiki. She quarreled with her powerful sister, Nāmaka, a goddess of the sea, and Nāmaka sent tidal waves to overflow Pele's lands and destroy her houses. Helped by her family Pele fought the sea goddess, but was defeated.

One of her brothers, the shark god, provided a canoe, and brothers and sisters sailed with Pele over the many-colored sea. Whenever they found an island Pele tried to make a home, but always Nāmaka followed and drove the family away.

At last they reached the island we call Kauaʻi. There Pele dug with her sacred digging stick, throwing up lava to form the hill still called Puʻuopele, The Hill of Pele. In the fire pit she had made, she and her brothers and sisters lived contentedly.

Alas! Nāmaka climbed to a high mountain top and, as she searched the sky, saw the glow of fire reflected on the clouds. "She lives! Pele lives!" the angry goddess shouted and rushed to the attack. Though brothers and sisters gathered about Pele and all fought bravely, they were defeated and fled before Nāmaka.

Pele and her family reached Oʻahu and once more Pele dug. She made a fire pit as she had done before, but salt water rose in it and drowned her fire. Today we call the pit she dug Salt Lake.

At Lēʻahi, which we call Diamond Head, Pele dug a fine crater, but once more water put out her fire. Again and again Pele tried—on Molokaʻi and West Maui. No better luck! Always salt water flowed in, and the fire was destroyed.

Finally, on the top of Haleakalā on Maui, a splendid pit was dug. Here the family lived, satisfied that they had a lasting home.

But again, from her lookout, Nāmaka saw smoke and glowing clouds. Once more she rushed to the attack. Pele had grown strong and confident. This time she fought single-handedly with her powerful sister. Long the battle raged, but at last Nāmaka won. She left the family mourning over Pele's death and returned to her own island in triumph. "Pele is no more!" she cried. "Her power is destroyed!"

Once again, from her point of lookout, Nāmaka searched the sky. What did she see? Over Mauna Loa, on the island of Hawai'i, dark smoke hung. The clouds above glowed red, and plainly the sea goddess saw among the clouds the form of a beautiful woman. "Pele lives!" she muttered. "She has become a goddess whom I can never kill."

The brothers and sisters also saw the lovely form among the clouds. "Pele lives!" they cried joyfully and joined Pele in her new home, the fire pit of Kīlauea. There the brothers tend her fires, and the sisters dance the *hula* or string *lehua lei*.

From Westervelt's "Hawaiian Legends of Volcanoes,"
taken originally from Hawaiian newspapers. Also from
"Hawaiian Antiquities" by Fornander.

FISH FROM FAR KAHIKI

Long ago canoes sailed back and forth from Hawai'i to Kahiki, the land that lies beyond the place where sky rests on the sea. Mo'ikeha was a voyager of that time who went to Far Kahiki and returned. He became ruling chief of Kaua'i and father of many sons.

One day Mo'ikeha said, "I long for *aku* and *'ōpelu* that swim in the sea-where-fish-do-run near my old home, Kahiki. Go, Kila my son, go to my father. Take to him my aloha and ask for fish."

So Kila traveled across the many-colored sea and found his grandfather. "Aloha!" he said. "My father sends his greeting."

"Who is your father?" the old man asked.

"Mo'ikeha."

The old eyes grew bright. "My son!" the old man cried. "He lives in that far land, Hawai'i. Tell me of him. Is he well? Has he food in plenty? Is he happy in that land?"

Kila answered in a chant:

"Mo'ikeha is chief of Kaua'i.
  He is happy in the sun that rises and sets,
  Happy in clouds that rest on the mountains,
  Happy in wind that sways the grasses,
  The wind which bends the trees.
  My father is happy with sticky *poi*,
  With seaweed and shrimp from the ocean.
  He is happy with breadfruit

46

Roasted in the *imu*,
In *'awa* root from the mountains.
My father swims in the surf.
He is happy in the love of my mother.
My father loves beautiful Kaua'i.
Kaua'i is home. He is chief."

The old man's eyes were shining. "That is a good chant," he said. "My son has much to make him happy. Is there anything he does not have? Is there any gift that I can send him?"

"Yes," Kila answered. "He longs for fish. He longs for *aku*, *'ōpelu* and other fish that swim near his old home. Send him some."

"It shall be so," the old man answered. "When you go home take those fish. Lead them through the sea as my gift to Mo'ikeha."

As Kila returned to Kaua'i, many fish followed his canoe and, ever since that day, they swim in the ocean about Hawai'i.

Translated by Mary Kawena Pūku'i from a Hawaiian newspaper

WHY THE MULLET SWIM AROUND OʻAHU

Each year the mullet swim from ʻEwa, past Waikīkī, around the end of Oʻahu, as far as Lāʻie. Then they swim back. "Why do they do this?" people wondered, and told this story to explain.

A young woman of ʻEwa had angered her family and had been sent away. She walked for many days, welcomed by strangers, yet longing for her home. At last she met a young farmer. Love grew between these two, they were married, and built a home at Lāʻie. There the young man made a fine taro patch, with sugar cane and bananas on its banks. He also had good sweet potatoes. With shellfish and seaweed from the reef his family were well fed, but they longed for fish. "The sea here at Lāʻie is empty," said the man, "and every day I think how good some fish would taste!"

"Yes," his wife answered. "At my childhood home in ʻEwa there were fish in plenty. Why don't you go there and get some for us?"

"Bring fish from ʻEwa!" the husband said. "Fresh fish would spoil! And a backload of dried fish would grow very heavy through many days of walking."

"Bring fish in the sea," answered his wife.

"Fish in the sea? I do not understand."

"My father is a man of wisdom," the young woman said. "He has power from the gods. It may be my parents have forgotten their anger toward me and will welcome you. Then my father will offer you some gift. Ask him for fish. He will show you a well-filled store house and

offer you salt fish. You must answer, 'I cannot carry such a heavy load. Give me fish in the sea.' "

The husband stared at his wife, puzzled. She smiled quietly. "Do as I say," she told him. "Then you will understand."

The young man trusted his wife and, though still puzzled, made the journey. It was a long, long journey following a trail beside the ocean. After many days he came to 'Ewa.

The wife's family had forgotten their anger and were eager for news of their daughter. They welcomed the young man and when they found he was their son-in-law they wailed with joy. He told of his wife, of their good lands and food plants.

"You two have prospered," said the father. "You have taro, potatoes, bananas, sugar cane. Is there anything you lack — any gift I can give my dear daughter and her husband?"

"We need fish," the young man answered. "Near Lā'ie there are none."

"You shall have fish," the father told him and led him to the store house. "Here are salt fish," he said. "Half of them are yours."

The young man remembered his wife's words. "How can I carry them so far?" he asked. "My back would break! Oh, give us fish in the sea."

"If my gods are willing," the father promised and went to pray.

The young man stayed in 'Ewa many days but nothing more was said about a gift. " I must return," he told the family. He was given a bundle of food for his journey, but nothing else.

"Take our aloha to your wife," the parents said. Then,

as the young man started, the father added, "You shall take fish in the sea."

As he walked the young man repeated the words, "fish in the sea." Over and over he said them, but could not understand.

He spent a night in Kou, at the mouth of the Nuʻuanu Stream, and found men busy fishing. "There is a run of mullet," he was told. All the village feasted.

"I wish we had such fish at Lāʻie," said the traveler. "Our sea is empty."

Next day he paused at Waikīkī. There too men were busy fishing. "There is a run of mullet," he was told.

He journeyed on. At every stop he heard of fish and always envied the fishermen. "At Lāʻie the sea is empty," he repeated many times.

At last he reached his home. His wife welcomed him gladly. He told her of her parents and of his journey. "Everywhere there were fish," he said. "Only here the sea is empty." His wife smiled wisely.

Next morning she woke him at sunrise. "They have come!" she said. "The mullet."

He hurried out. It was true! The bay was silver with mullet. "How strange!" he said. "The sea is no longer empty!"

"These are the fish you brought," answered his wife. "My father prayed, and the gods sent the mullet to follow you."

The young man hurried to join his neighbors in fishing. So that was it! At Kou, at Waikīkī, everywhere along his journey men had caught fish because the mullet followed him! The young man thanked the gods.

Translated by Mary Kawena Pūkuʻi from a Hawaiian newspaper

HANAKAHI'S FISHPOND

The great gods lived on islands which floated among the clouds, but they sometimes came to visit homes of men. Once Kāne and Kanaloa came upon a pointed cloud. They reached O'ahu near 'Ewa and walked along the hot, dry trail. "O brother, I am hungry!" Kanaloa said.

Now 'awa is loved by gods as well as men and is both drink and food to them. But 'awa juice must be mixed with water. As he looked about, Kāne saw nothing but dry land and salty sea. He struck the dry land with his staff, and water flowed. The gods mixed 'awa, drank, and felt new strength to journey on. Again and again as they journeyed Kāne struck the earth, and springs gushed out.

At last the two reached the entrance to Pu'uloa which we call Pearl Harbor. They swam and surfed, then rested on the sand. "Once again I am hungry," said Kanaloa with a laugh.

"There is a fisherman's home," his brother answered. "Shall we go there and ask for food?"

"Those houses are small and poor," said Kanaloa, "and the man's canoe is worn. He is one who works hard and may have little food for guests."

"Let us see," Kāne answered wisely, and the two drew near the little home.

They heard the voice of someone praying,

"O unknown gods,
Here is 'awa drink,

Here are fish and *poi*.
I pray you take this food
And bless my fishing."

When his prayer was ended the fisherman looked out and saw the strangers. "Aloha!" he called in welcome. "I have *'awa* ready. I have cooked fish and pounded *poi*. Come in and eat with Hanakahi."

The gods drank and ate. "We heard you pray, O Hanakahi," Kāne said. "We heard you offer food and drink to unknown gods. We are those gods who shall no longer be unknown to you. We are Kāne and Kanaloa. Pray to us by name. Now we must go, but in the morning we shall return once more."

"He is a good man," Kanaloa said as they went out.

"Yes, a good man," his brother answered. "He paddles far to sea for fish and comes home tired. Yet he mixes *'awa* and prepares food for the gods. Let us build a fishpond for him."

"Yes, let us build a pond here in the ocean's edge and fill it with good fish."

By morning the pond was built and filled with fish. Then Kāne prayed,

"Fish shall come in at this pond's gate,
But no fish shall go out.
Neither shall fish go out over the wall.
This pond shall be always full of fish.
Never again shall Hanakahi grow tired
With long paddling."

When morning came they showed the pond to Hanakahi. "It is for you," they told him, "for you and your children that you may have all the fish you need."

53

The two gods climbed a hill and looked over the landlocked water of Puʻuloa. They looked over the plains and mountains. "Hawaiʻi is a good land," they told each other as they returned to their island in the clouds.

Long the family of Hanakahi took fish from that pond, and long men drank from springs left by the gods.

Translated by Mary Kawena Pūkuʻi from a Hawaiian newspaper

MAKUA'S PRAYER

Makua was a farmer of windward Oʻahu, but he was more than that. He was also a *kahuna*, or priest. He had been trained in Far Kahiki and served the *heiau* wisely and well.

His son was an earnest young man who worked early and late on the farm and who learned all that his father could teach. But Makua wanted his son to have power and wisdom greater than his own. Again and again he prayed,

"O Kāne, O Kanaloa,
  Be my son's teachers
  That he may become
  A *kahuna*, wiser, greater
  Than his father."

Had the gods heard his prayer? Makua wondered.

One day as he prepared the evening meal, Makua heard voices outside his eating house. Two men were coming up the trail. "Aloha!" Makua called to them. "You are welcome. Come in and eat with us." He set food before the men, *ʻawa*, *poi*, bananas, and shell fish from the reef. Then as was his custom he made offering and prayed to Kāne and Kanaloa. After his prayer he and his guests ate and rested.

Darkness was coming as the strangers rose to leave. "Do not go," Makua begged. "Mats are ready in our sleeping house. The trail is steep and dark. Stay here until the morning."

"Our way will not be dark," the strangers answered.

Suddenly Makua knew his guests. "Kāne and Kana-loa!" he whispered.

"Yes. We have heard your prayers. In good time we shall answer them. We shall send a messenger for your son to bring him to our land where we shall be his teachers. Then he will return, wiser than his father as you have prayed. Be patient for in good time our messenger will come." Makua's heart was full of joy.

But the time was long. Years passed, and no messenger appeared. Had the gods forgotten? Makua waited patiently and prayed. There seemed to be no answer to his prayer.

One day as father and son worked in the taro patch they heard the sound of shouting coming faintly from the beach. The young man raised his head to listen. "What is it?" he wondered. "I must go to the beach and learn why people shout."

"Wait!" said Makua. "Tonight our neighbors will return and we shall hear."

They did indeed! The neighbors talked excitedly. "A whale!" they said. "A whale has come ashore. Its tail rests on the beach and it lies there quiet, washed by the waves."

"Dead?" asked Makua's son.

"We do not know. It is still as in death, yet seems alive. We dare not cut the flesh to take it to the chief."

"Why was there shouting?"

"Boys climbed upon the whale. They ran the length of the great creature, then plunged into the sea as from a cliff."

"What glorious sport!" the young man cried. "I am going to the beach tomorrow to see the whale, to run along its length and jump into deep water. Such a chance may never come again!"

But Makua was unwilling. Something seemed to tell him of danger to his son.

Days passed. Each evening neighbors told them of the whale. It still lay quiet as in death. Still men and boys were jumping from its body. "I must see it, Father!" the young man said again.

Makua feared to have him go, yet saw no reason for his fear. "Yes, go, my son," he said at last. Gladly the young man gathered flowers.

Next morning, decked with the *lei* which he had made and wearing a new *malo,* he hurried to the beach. There lay the whale! Makua's son gazed long and touched the firm sides with his hands. At last he climbed, ran the length of the great beast, and leaped into the sea. Truly it was glorious sport! Again and again, with others, he ran, jumped, and swam back to the beach to run and jump again.

Suddenly there was a shout of warning, "*E!* Jump! Jump quickly!" Makua's son seemed to feel an earthquake. The whale was moving. Men jumped this way and that fleeing from it. Only Makua's son stood for a moment frightened, not knowing what to do. In that moment the whale plunged from the beach and swam more swiftly than a canoe can sail before the wind.

Makua heard wailing voices. Then his neighbors came. "He is gone!" they told Makua. "The whale swam away. Your son was on its back. We saw him clinging there as the whale disappeared."

"Gone forever!" the father cried. "Oh, I begged him not to go down to the beach. I knew some danger waited there. *Auē! Auē!*"

For days Makua mourned. Then came a dream. In sleep his gods, Kāne and Kanaloa, stood beside his mats. "Do not mourn," they said. "At last your prayer is answered. Our messenger came for your son and brought him safely to our land. We are his teachers. After a time he will return to you."

And so it was. The son returned at last with wisdom and great power. Makua lived to see his boy a very great *kahuna*, a wise leader. And Makua thanked the gods.

Told by Mary Kawena Pūkuʻi

THE SHARK GUARDIAN

This is a story of the days when Mary Kawena Pūkuʻi was a little girl in Kaʻū on Hawaiʻi. One very rainy day she got to thinking of a certain kind of fish. "I want *nenue* fish," she said.

"Hush child," her mother answered. "We have none."

"But I am hungry for *nenue* fish!" the little girl repeated and began to cry.

"Stop your crying!" said another woman crossly. "Don't you see we can't go fishing today? Just look out at the pouring rain. No one can get you *nenue* fish. Keep still!"

The little girl went off into a corner and cried softly so that no one should hear, "I do want *nenue* fish! Why can't someone get it for me?"

Her aunt came in out of the rain. It was Kawena's merry young aunt who was always ready for adventure. "What is the matter with the child?" she was asking. "The skies are shedding tears enough, Kawena. Why do you add more?"

"I want *nenue* fish," the little girl whispered.

"Then you shall have some. The rain is growing less. We will go to my uncle."

In a moment the little girl had put on her raincoat, and the two were walking through the lessening rain. It was fun to be out with this merry aunt, fun to slip on wet rock, and shake the drops from dripping bushes.

At last they reached the uncle's cave. "Aloha!" the old man called. "What brings you two this rainy morning?"

"The grandchild is hungry for *nenue* fish," Kawena's aunt replied.

"And *nenue* fish she shall have," said the old man. Net in hand he climbed the rocks above his cave home. Kawena and her aunt watched him as he stood looking out over the bay. He stood there like a man of wood until the little girl grew tired watching. The rain had stopped and sunlight touched the silent figure. Why didn't he do something? Why didn't he get her fish? Why did he stand there so long — so long?

Suddenly he moved. With quick leaps he made his way to the beach and waded out. Kawena and her aunt hurried after him and saw him draw his net about some fish and lift them from the water. Just as the girl and woman reached the beach the old man held up a fish. "The first for you, old one," he said and threw the fish into the bay. A shark rose from the water to seize it. "These for the grandchild," the old man added. He was still speaking to the shark as he gave four fish to Kawena.

The little girl took her fish, but her wondering eyes were following the shark as he swam away.

"That is our guardian," the uncle said. He too was watching the shark until it disappeared.

"Tell her about our guardian," said the aunt. "Kawena ought to know that story."

The uncle led them back to his cave. There, dry and comfortable, they sat looking down at the beach and the bay. "It was from those rocks that I first saw him." The uncle began, his eyes on rocks below.

"One day, many years ago, I found my older brother lying on the sand. For a moment I thought that he was dead. Then he opened his eyes and saw me. 'Bring *'awa*

and bananas,' he whispered. I stood looking at him, not understanding his strange words. After a bit he opened his eyes again and saw me still beside him. " '*Awa* and bananas!' he repeated. 'Get them quickly.'

"As I started away I saw him pull himself to his feet, holding onto a rock. He looked out over the bay and called, 'Wait, O my guardian! The boy has gone for food.' Then he sank back upon the sand. I looked out into the bay, but saw no one.

"I got '*awa* drink and ripe bananas and brought them to my brother. He pulled himself weakly to his feet once more and moved out onto those rocks, motioning me to bring the food. He called again and his voice was stronger. 'O my guardian, come! Here is '*awa* drink! Here are bananas! Come and eat.'

"Suddenly a large shark appeared just below the rocks on which we stood. As my brother raised the wooden bowl of '*awa,* the great fish opened his mouth. Carefully my brother poured the drink into that open mouth till all was gone. Then he peeled the bananas one by one and tossed them to the shark, until the great fish was satisfied. 'I thank you, O my guardian!' Brother said. 'Today you saved my life. Come here when you are hungry.' The shark turned and swam away.

"While my brother rested on the sand he told me his adventure. His canoe had been caught in a squall and overturned. He was blinded by rain and waves and could not find the canoe. It must have drifted away. The waves broke over him and he thought the end had come.

"Then he felt himself on something firm. 'A rock!' he thought and clung to it. Suddenly he felt himself moving through the waves and knew that he was riding on the back of a great shark and clinging to his fin. He was frightened, but kept his hold.

"The storm passed on, and my brother saw the beach. The shark swam into shallow water, and Brother stumbled up the sand. It was there I found him.

"He never forgot that shark. Often I have seen him standing on the rocks above this cave with 'awa and bananas ready. Sometimes he called. Sometimes he waited quietly until the shark saw him and came. Sometimes the shark drove a small school of fish into the bay as you saw just now. My brother caught some and shared them with the shark.

"The time came when my brother was very sick. Before he died he beckoned to me. 'My guardian,' he whispered. 'You must give food to the one that saved my life.'

"I have not forgotten, and the shark does not forget. I feed him 'awa and bananas, and he sometimes drives fish into my net. Today he wanted *nenue* fish and put the thought of them into your mind. Always remember our guardian, Kawena."

Kawena Pūku'i is a woman now, but she has never forgotten the shark guardian.

Told by Mary Kawena Pūku'i

THE TREE WITH SILVERY LEAVES

Long, long ago our islands came up from the sea and lay barren — mountains and plains and beaches. The sun god had not yet come from the ocean. Only moon and stars gave light. The tree god came and sat upon the sandy shore where a stream entered the sea. He took white sand, moistened with water from the stream, and made seeds of many kinds. When these were dry he planted them. Some he planted near the beach, some on the level plain, others in gulches or on black lava slopes.

Tiny trees sprang up with many-colored leaves. For a little time these trees grew, but the dim light of moon and stars was not enough. They sickened and withered away. The tree god searched on shore, plain, and mountain slope. "My trees are dead," he said. "They need the sun." But still he searched and in small gulches found growing trees. Lighted only by moon and stars these little trees had flourished, and their leaves were like moonlight seen through floating clouds or reflected on still water.

Kukui trees still grow in gulches and on mountain slopes. Lighted now by the sun their small new leaves are green. As the leaves grow they turn a silvery color so that a *kukui* grove looks as if lighted by the moon. The trees seem to remember it was the moon which gave light to their ancestors.

From a legend told by a Hawaiian boy and written by MacCaugh for "Paradise of the Pacific." Used by permission.

HI‘IAKA'S PĀ‘Ū

Pele came to the beach to surf. In her arms she carried Hi‘iaka, her dearly-loved baby sister. She laid the sleepy baby on the sand. "Lie here," she whispered, "where this rock will shelter you from sun and wind. Soon I shall return, O little Hi‘iaka."

The surf was high that day. Pele swam out, then caught a great wave and came rushing in, standing on her long board and shouting in her joy. Again and again she rode the waves, not once remembering the sleeping child.

At last, a little tired, she waded toward the beach. "The sun!" she thought suddenly. "It is overhead. This must be noon, for my shadow is below me. That rock can give no shelter now. Oh, the poor baby lying in the burning sun!" And Pele hurried to the place where she had left her sister.

But all was well with the little one, for a vine which grew upon the rock had seen her. As the rock's shadow grew shorter and shorter the vine had stretched out its tendrils and formed a shelter over the child, just as a loving mother spreads her *pā‘ū* to shelter her little one.* Only tiny rays of sunshine could slip between the leaves to rest gently on the baby. Pele was glad and gave the vine the name it bears today, Hi‘iaka's *pā‘ū*.

Told by Mary Kawena Pūku‘i

*A *pā‘ū* was a strip of kapa which a woman wrapped about her to form a skirt.

66

THE GIRL WHO LIVED WITH THE MOʻO

(A legend of Waimea Valley, Kauaʻi)

"O Mother, play with me!"

"I have no time. See, I am making dye to dye this *kapa*. Play by yourself."

The little girl began to whimper. When she saw her mother still busy with the dye she started toward the sweet-potato patch. "Father," she called as she came near. "Come and play with me."

"I am weeding the potatoes," her father said. "I have no time to play."

Again the child began to whimper. "You don't love me," she said crossly. "No one loves me. I guess I'll go away."

Her father went on weeding.

Looking about, the child saw a great lizard sunning on the rock above the waterfall. "The *moʻo* would be kinder to me than you are," she said.

Still her father did not answer, but went on pulling weeds.

"The *moʻo* has time," the little girl remarked. "He doesn't work. He has time to play with me."

"Then go and live with him!" exclaimed the father, annoyed by the child's teasing.

There was no more crying that afternoon. The parents were glad their child had gone off to play. She was a bother with her whimpering and teasing when they had work to do. But as darkness fell they looked for her. They called and hunted. No one had seen her. All night the parents searched.

In the morning a neighbor came. "I have seen your child," he told them. "She seems safe and happy. Come." He led them toward their garden. From there they could see the waterfall, and on the rocks above it, touched by the morning sun, lay the great *mo'o.* Nestled happily against him they saw their child.

The father called to her. Startled by the sound the great lizard leaped over the fall and disappeared into a cave behind it. The child ran to a small opening above the fall, and she too disappeared into the cave.

"Don't worry!" said the mother. "She will come for food."

But the child did not come. Often they saw her sunning beside the *mo'o* or quietly playing with him. Since she seemed well fed and happy, they let her stay.

But as she grew they said, "That is not a good life for a girl. She must learn the work of women. She must have friends about her and learn their ways." Again they called to her and urged her to return to them. But always, startled by the calls, the *mo'o* leaped over the fall and disappeared into the cave while the girl ran to the smaller opening above.

At last the parents went to a *kahuna.* The father followed his advice and brought a net. As the strange friends lay sunning on the rock he stole behind them, fastened the net in the small opening, then hid.

The mother called, "O daughter, we want you to come home!"

The *mo'o* leaped over the fall and disappeared behind it. The girl ran to the small opening, but was stopped by the net. In a moment the father had her in his arms.

The family moved from Waimea Valley to the village. At first their girl was a wild, unwilling prisoner. But soon she came to love the sports and friendship of other girls. She learned to work beside her mother and was content. But all her life people called her the girl who lived with the *moʻo*.

Told by Rice in "Hawaiian Legends" and used by permission of the Bernice P. Bishop Museum

HŌLUA MANU

Manu broke off the top of a ti plant and started up the trail. "Where are you going?" called his mother.

"Up the trail," the boy answered carelessly.

"To slide?" she questioned. "Oh, not on that steep slope! Manu, you may be killed! Don't slide there!"

"There is no danger, Mother! The slide is glorious! When I slide there I feel that I am truly Manu, the bird."

"No!" said his mother firmly. "Use the hill below."

"That is a slide for children!" grumbled Manu, but he turned and took the downward trail. He reached the slide, a long, sandy slope. He sat on his bunch of ti leaves, holding the stalk firmly between his knees, and down he went.

When he reached the bottom he threw away his ti as he said crossly, "That slide was fun while I was a child, but now it is too slow."

He climbed the trail and passed his home. His mother was busy now and did not see him. The boy broke a fresh stalk of ti and climbed on to the slide he loved. There he paused, looking down. "So that is what she's done!" he said aloud. "She has asked my father to block my slide with those two rocks. Well," he stood looking carefully, "I can avoid them."

He seated himself firmly on the ti, gave a push and flew down the steep slope of the cliff. With a skillful movement he sent himself around the smaller rock. Then he flew through the air in a mighty leap over the larger one. He landed with a bump and slid to the level place below.

He rubbed his back, for the jar of his leap had hurt. Then he climbed to the rocks. "You hurt me!" he said angrily to the larger rock. "Jumping over you gave me an awful bump. I'll give you a bump, you great rock!" And with a mighty heave he rolled it into the Waimea Stream below. Then he rolled the smaller rock down also. "I won't slide here again," he thought. "I'll find a place where Mother will not see and worry."

He started up Waimea Valley to the Canyon. "Here," he said, "here is a slide for Manu." The boy scrambled to the top of a great cliff, broke off some ti, and made ready for his slide. For a moment he sat poised, looking down, then quickly, before fear should overcome him, pushed himself over the edge.

Oh, the swift and glorious slide! "Now I am indeed a bird!" thought the boy. He reached the bottom and climbed up to slide again and yet again.

Men still point to the rocks that Manu threw out of his way into the Waimea Stream. And the steepest cliff of the canyon wall still bears the name Hōlua Manu, The Slide of the Bird.

Told by Rice in "Hawaiian Legends" and used by permission of the Bernice P. Bishop Museum

THE COCONUT WHISTLE

Not far from the Waiʻanae Mountains on Oʻahu lived a boy who could not talk. Thoughts rose in him as water rises in a spring, but he could not speak his thoughts. He could not tell his family when he was sad. He could not share with them his jokes and fun.

Often his heart was heavy, and his family saw his sadness. "It is because he cannot talk," they said. His grandfather added, "He must make music. That will tell his thoughts." So the grandfather sent a servant into the forest to make a nose flute, and taught his grandson how to play it. The boy played so well men stopped their work to listen. Yet the nose flute did not satisfy him, for it could not tell his thoughts.

"He must have the coconut whistle," said his grandmother.

"That sacred whistle?" his mother asked. "But that is guarded by two watchers. No one can get that whistle."

The grandmother smiled wisely and shook her little blossoming tree until two blossoms flew from it and floated off, carried by the wind. On and on they flew till they were near the place where the coconut whistle was guarded. The watchers saw those blossoms floating like gay butterflies, and went to catch them, not thinking of the whistle they should guard.

When they were gone a small bird came, seized the whistle and flew back to the boy. "This will speak your thoughts," the wise bird told him. "Your grandmother sent me for it."

The boy put the whistle to his lips and blew. Oh, the music that he made! All his thoughts came bubbling up, and the whistle spoke them. Now he could share both joy and sorrow with his family. He was no longer sad.

Translated by Mary Kawena Pūku'i from a Hawaiian newspaper

THE SWEET POTATO THIEF

Owl was a farmer of Kohala. Every night he worked in his sweet potato patch, for the light of day blinded his eyes. He dug, he planted slips, and in a dry time brought water to his growing vines. With pride he saw potatoes pushing from the earth.

Then one night he saw that some of his young potatoes had been pulled and eaten. "Rat!" he thought. "That great Rat is too lazy to make a garden for himself and comes to steal my food. I'll watch for him."

Though he watched every night Owl saw nothing of Rat. "He knows that I am watching and does his stealing somewhere else," Owl said at last and saw his vines grow strong and green with great potatoes pushing from the earth.

So many big potatoes! "I wonder if my storehouse can hold them all," thought Owl happily as he came out to harvest them. He seized a big potato top and pulled. Up it came in a moment—a potato top but nothing more! The marks of gnawing teeth showed what had happened. Owl pulled another potato top and still another. All the same! Rat had tunneled under the patch and eaten all.

Sadly Owl filled his gourd with sweet potato tops. "One meal!" he sadly thought. "Or maybe two—two meals from my fine big garden!" He built a fire and heated stones. He washed and wrapped the pieces of potato, packed them in the *imu* with hot stones, covered the *imu,* and went about other work.

R. BURNINGHAM

"There is enough for two good meals!" he thought as he uncovered the *imu* and sniffed the good smell of roasted potatoes. But there was little there besides the smell! Rat had come while Owl was away. He had uncovered the *imu*, taken all the food but a few scraps, and carefully put back the covering. Wicked Rat!

Owl ate a few bits of potato and put the rest away thinking, "I'll have one more small meal tomorrow."

But when tomorrow came the gourd was empty. That thieving Rat had made a hole and stolen the last bits of sweet potato! For Owl nothing was left except starvation. He grew weak and hollow-eyed, too weak to hunt for roots and fern shoots. "Soon I shall die," he muttered.

It was then Hawk visited him. "What's the matter, Owl?" Hawk asked surprised. "You look sick."

"I am," the other answered sadly, "sick with hunger."

"Hunger? I thought you were a farmer!"

"I was. There was no better farmer in all Kohala. I had a big patch of sweet potatoes. But who ate them all? Rat! That thief gnawed every potato. Then he opened the *imu* and ate. He gnawed a hole in my gourd bowl and took the last scraps. Nothing is left for me but death."

"Why don't you kill Rat?" Hawk asked.

"How can I, now I am so weak?"

"Come along with me," said Hawk. "I'll do the killing. You will only have to help a little." His friend's words gave Owl new strength, so that he managed to hop along to Rat's house.

Rat saw them and came out to welcome them. He thought his stealing was so clever that Owl had not suspected him. Before he could say, "Aloha!" Hawk had pounced and was ready to eat him.

76

"Don't eat him!" Owl shouted. "Tear him to pieces."

Hawk tore Rat into small pieces. That is why rats, today, are small and why they have no love for owls and hawks. But they are the same thieving fellows as the big rat who ate Owl's sweet potatoes. As for Owl, he is no longer a farmer, but a hunter of rats and mice.

From a Hawaiian newspaper translated by Mary Kawena Pūku'i
and "Folk Tales from Hawai'i" by Green

"HELP YOURSELF"

Keoha, a canoe-maker of Hilo, had come to Puna. The trail was long, the day hot, and now Keoha stood looking longingly at a bunch of coconuts in a tree top.

"Aloha, stranger! What are you looking at?" A fisherman had stopped beside Keoha.

"Those coconuts. Their cool milk would moisten my dry throat, and the meat of a tender young nut would taste very good."

"Come with me," the Puna fisherman invited. "I have many coconuts and shall give you all you want. Come to my home."

Keoha went gladly. The walk was long, but the Hilo man thought eagerly of the good food and drink that he could find. He hurried.

At last the fisherman stopped beside tall coco palms. "There are coconuts, stranger," he said smiling. "Help yourself."

There they were indeed! High in the tree tops! Years ago Keoha could have climbed one of these coco palms, but not now. "Thank you. I am no longer thirsty," he answered as he walked away.

A little later as he passed a group of houses the canoe-maker was called in. Boys climbed trees for coconuts, and Keoha and his hosts ate tender young nuts and drank cool milk. The stranger was refreshed and very grateful. These men became his friends.

The canoe-maker, however, did not forget the fisherman. "Some day I shall repay his kindness," he told himself.

Years later his chance came. The Puna man walked into the shed where Keoha was polishing a canoe. "My small fishing canoe was injured in a storm," he said. "I need another. Have you one?"

Keoha looked around. "Not here. These are all promised," he answered, speaking truly. "But there is one in the forest. Meet me early tomorrow, and I shall show you."

Carrying food and water the two took the trail. The day grew hot, but they climbed on for the fisherman was eager to see his new canoe.

At last they reached the part of the forest where tall koa trees grew — the strong trees whose trunks can stand the beat of waves and scratch of pebbles. Keoha looked from one to another of the great trees as he said, "Here are many canoes. Help yourself."

Told by Mary Kawena Pūku'i

THE PUNAHOU SPRING

There was a dry time on Oʻahu. No rain fell, streams dried, and many springs ceased to flow. It was a hungry time, for gardens too were dry.

In Mānoa Valley at the foot of Rocky Hill lived an old couple. This dry time was very hard for these old folks. Mūkākā, the husband, must walk far up the valley to get ti roots and ferns for food. Kealoha, his wife, must walk each day to Kamōʻiliʻili where a spring still flowed. There she must fill her water gourds and carry them up the long rough trail back to her home.

One day the way seemed longer and harder than ever. Kealoha rested on a rock. "I can't go on!" she thought, "I can't carry the water all that way." But then she thought, "I must! We must have water." She rose and lifted her carrying pole. Wind swept about her, filling her eyes with dust. It almost blew her off her feet, yet she struggled on.

When she reached home she found Mūkākā there before her preparing food. But Kealoha was too tired to eat. She lay upon her mats and cried with weariness. At last she slept and dreamed. In her dream a man stood beside her mats. "Why do you cry?" he asked her. "Because I am so weary," she replied. "Each day I walk to Kamōʻiliʻili and fill my water gourds. The trail is hot, dusty, and long. I am too tired!"

"You need not go again," answered the man. "Close to your home, under the *hala* tree, there is a spring. There fill your gourds." The man was gone.

When morning came Kealoha told her dream, but her husband hardly listened. "An empty dream," he said, "that came to you because of thirst." He started for the upland.

She watched him, thinking, "He is bent and feeble. Why does he not listen to my words, pull up the *hala,* and open our own spring?" But when she went to look at the tree, she doubted. Under it the ground was dry and hard. Surely there was no water there. It was an empty dream!

That night Mūkākā dreamed. A man stood by his mats and spoke to him. "There is a spring," he said, "under the *hala* which grows beside your home. You must pull up that tree. Go catch red fish, wrap it in ti leaves, heat the *imu,* and cook your fish. Make offering and pray for strength to uproot the tree. Then you will find the spring."

Mūkākā sat up in the early dawn. "The same dream!" he thought, "It came to Kealoha, now to me. The god of the spring has come to help us in our need. I must obey him."

In the cool of the morning Mūkākā and a friend went to Waikīkī for fish. The fish came quickly to their hooks, and some of them were red. "The god is with us," said Mūkākā and hurried home to heat the *imu.* When the food was cooked he made offering and prayed.

After they had eaten he said to his friend, "My wife and I each had a dream. Two nights ago Kealoha dreamed, and last night the same dream came to me. A god stood by my mats and said, 'A spring is here. Pull up that *hala* tree which grows beside your home, and water will flow.' O my friend, I have offered red fish to that god and prayed for strength. We both are strong with food. Now help me pull."

The two men grasped the *hala* tree. Their muscles strained, and sweat poured down their bodies. They stopped for breath then pulled again, but still the tree stood firm. The friend looked at the dry earth. "No water here!" he said. "You dreamed of water because of your great thirst."

"The dream was true!" Mūkākā answered. "Twice the god stood by our mats. He spoke to Kealoha and to me. His words were true." The old man prayed again. "Let us try once more," he said. "This time we shall succeed."

Once more they struggled with the tree. "It moves!" they shouted and pulled again with more strength than before. The tree came from the ground, and they saw water moistening the earth—a little water. Mūkākā ran for his digging stick and cleared away earth and stones. A tiny stream gushed out.

For a moment the three stared in wonder. Then Kealoha shouted, "*Ka puna hou!* The new spring!"

Now there was water for all that neighborhood. No more long walks to the Kamōʻiliʻili spring! Water flowed steadily. Men dug and let the water soak the ground. They built walls and planted taro. Through these taro patches the spring water flowed, and fish were brought to flourish there. Fish and taro grew, and so the spring gave food as well as water. The people thanked the gods that now their life was good.

Long afterward a school was built beside that spring. It bears the name that Kealoha gave in her glad cry, and its seal is a *hala* tree. "This school shall be a spring of wisdom," said its founders. "As the *hala* tree stands firm through wind or storm, so shall the children of this school stand strong and brave through joy and sorrow. As the *hala* has many uses, so shall these children be useful to Hawai'i."

Translated by Mary Kawena Pūku'i from a Hawaiian newspaper

THE WATERS OF HA‘O

The caretakers of Kewalo Spring saw two children coming wearily along the trail. They saw the little girl stumble and fall. The boy, a little older, helped her to her feet and seemed to urge her to reach the spring. "Those two have been neglected," one man remarked. "They look half starved, and their *kapa* is soiled and torn."

"May we have water?" asked the boy when the spring was reached at last. "The trail is hot, and our water gourd is empty." The little girl sank down on the grass as if she could go no farther. When her brother had filled his gourd she drank eagerly, then snuggled against him and fell asleep.

The kind-hearted caretakers fed the children. Later they took them into the sleeping house "These two must come from some poor home where relatives are old or lazy," they said to one another. "Here they can rest."

Next morning the men woke early and went to tend their garden. As the sun rose mist blew from the mountains, and over the sleeping house a rainbow hung. "A rainbow!" said one. "Over our sleeping house! No chief—"

"The children!" his companion answered. "Who can they be?"

That day the caretakers of the spring were greatly puzzled. The children stayed as if glad of food and rest, but they did not tell their names or family, and no one came for them. Should the boy and girl be treated as young chiefs? A rainbow was a chiefly sign. The men were puzzled.

The children stayed for several days. They were quiet and often slept. The little girl especially seemed always tired.

One evening, after they had entered the sleeping house, a farmer from Makiki stopped at the spring to drink and talk. "The children of Ha‘o have run away," he said.

"The children of the district chief?"

"Yes. Their mother died some time ago, and the new chiefess has no love for them. When Ha‘o, their father, is away she gives them little food and she is always scolding."

"No wonder they have run away!"

"Yes," said the man. "They are good children, a boy and little sister. We hoped that they might find a better home, but now the chiefess is sending men to hunt for them. She has seen a rainbow down this way and says it is the rainbow of those children. Her men will find and punish those who help them."

The caretakers of the spring looked at each other. "It may be those who help the children will not give them up," said one in a determined voice.

"No common man can stand against the anger of that chiefess," was the answer. After the visitor had gone the two sat talking in low voices, trying to make a plan to hide the children. At last they slept.

When all was still the boy, who like his father was called Ha‘o, rose from his mats. He took his sister in his arms and staggered with her into the moonlight. There he set her on her feet. As she woke she began to cry, but the brother hushed her. "You are the daughter of a

85

chief," he whispered. "You must be brave. Come."

"Where are we going?" she asked. "I don't want to go. I'm sleepy."

"By and by we shall sleep," he answered. "The chiefess is sending men to get us. Do you want to be scolded and punished again? Besides if she finds us here she will be cruel to those who helped us. Come, O my sister. We must be far away."

"Yes," the little girl agreed, "she must not find us." They followed the moonlit trail across the plain toward Kou at the mouth of the Nu'uanu Stream. Several times the little girl said, "I am very tired," but walked bravely on. Suddenly she stopped. "I am thirsty," she whispered to her brother. "O Ha'o, I must have a drink."

Ha'o shook his water gourd, but heard no sound. "It is empty," he said. "I thought only that we must get away and forgot to fill my gourd. Let us go on and find another spring."

But now the little girl was crying with weariness and thirst. When she tripped over a stone and fell, Ha'o gave up, made her comfortable on dry grass and patted her gently until she slept. But the boy did not sleep. He too was tired and thirsty and he was deeply troubled. Where should they go? How could he get food for his sister? And water? They must have water!

With a last thirsty thought he fell asleep and, in a dream, he heard a call, "Ha'o, O Ha'o!" It was his mother's voice. He saw her standing beside him just as she used to do. "You are thirsty, my children," she said. "Pull up the bush close to your feet." Then the form faded, and Ha'o woke.

"It was a dream!" he thought. "Our mother came in a dream. I must obey her words." He took hold of the

R. BURNINGHAM

bush growing near him, but it hurt his hands. He took big leaves for a protection, braced himself and pulled with all his might. Up came the bush and, where it had been, water flowed. A spring! Haʻo filled the gourd, then woke his sister and gave her a cool drink. "It is the water of the gods," he said. Then he too drank. "Our mother watches over us," he whispered and, comforted, slept soundly.

When next the children woke the sun was shining. Men stood looking at them and at the spring—their father's men! Haʻo sprang up and greeted them with joy. He told them of his dream, and all drank from the spring.

"Come home," the men said. "Your father longs for you."

"The chiefess?" asked the girl in a troubled voice.

"Have no more fear of her," the men replied. "The gods showed you this spring because of their love for you. You are their chosen ones, and the chiefess will not dare to do you harm."

For many years that spring flowed. Its waters bubbled into a pool edged by ferns and fragrant vines. At one time a house was built over the pool to make it the bathing place for a chiefess. She too was Haʻo, a descendant of the one who found the spring. She was a high chiefess and very sacred, very *kapu*. No one except her family and servants might even look at her. She might not set foot upon the ground. If she did so, the place where she had stepped would be *kapu* and no common person could step on it. So her servants brought her to the spring in a *mānele*, curtained with fine *kapa*. She bathed in the fern-edged pool and then was carried home. Because it was the bathing place of this young chiefess the spring came to be called The Water of Ha'o.

That spring no longer flows for a city has grown all about it, and people pipe their water from deep wells and mountain reservoirs. Today a church stands near the place where the thirsty children drank and where the *kapu* chiefess bathed. The church bears the name of the spring, The Water of Ha'o, Kawaiaha'o.

The first part of this story was told by Emma K. Nākuina in "The Friend"; the second part is from a translation by Mary Kawena Pūku'i from a Hawaiian newspaper.

THE SPRINGS OF KOʻOLAU LOA

Two strangers came to Koʻolau Loa on Oʻahu, two tall fine-looking men. The eyeball of the sun was sinking in the west, and the men were thirsty and tired. "Here are good houses," said one, "and over there is a spring. Let us ask here for drink and rest."

"*E!*" the men called. "Have you water for thirsty travelers?"

Two old people came to the doorway. "We have no water for strangers," said the man. The travelers glanced toward the spring which bubbled out and formed a little stream. "That is only enough for ourselves," the old man added quickly.

"Be on your way!" called the old woman. "We want no strangers here." And the two stood blocking their doorway.

Without a word the tall men walked away. Close to the shore they found another home. "These houses are small," one of the men remarked. "No room for strangers here! And I don't see any spring."

"Aloha!" called a friendly voice. "You are welcome! Come and eat." An old man hurried toward them from the little home.

"We are thirsty," said the travelers, "but you have no spring."

"Oh yes, we have a spring," the old man answered. "It is in the ocean's edge, and the water is a little salty, but better than none. I'll fill the water gourds." He led the strangers to his eating house, brought water, and set food before them.

When they had eaten, he led them to the sleeping house. "Your mats are ready," he told them.

The two looked about. "Those are your mats," they answered. "Where shall you sleep?"

"Right here," said the old woman quickly, showing them a mat laid on the floor. "We like a cool place when the night is warm."

"You are kind," the tall men told her. "We hope you will not feel the hardness of the pebbles underneath your mat."

The old folks did not feel the pebbles. They slept well and when they woke their guests were gone. "Why did they leave so early?" asked the man in disappointment. "I should have given them food." He went to fill the water gourd and gave his wife a drink.

She tasted, then looked at him in surprise. "Where did this water come from?"

"From our spring, there in the ocean's edge. Is the water very salty?"

"It is not salty at all," she told him. "Taste it. It is cool and fresh." He tasted, and the two looked at each other wondering.

Later they heard that the spring nearer the mountains had turned salty in the night. That was the spring of which the owner said, "Its water is only enough for ourselves."

"Our visitors were two gods," the kind man said to his wife. "It was well I gave them drink and food."

"You did for them what you do for all who come," his wife replied. "Now we shall have good water for our guests."

91

The water from these springs still flows as the gods willed. The water some distance from the ocean is a little salty, while the spring in the ocean's edge gives water which is fresh and cool.

Told to Mary Kawena Pūku'i by a native of Hau'ula
and previously printed in "The Legend of Kawelo"
by Green and Pūku'i

WATER WITHOUT SOURCE

For many years people had lived in Hawai'i *nei*. Its streams and springs gave water, food plants grew and life was good. Then, to a part of windward O'ahu, there came a time of drought. No rain fell, springs became dry, there was no water in the streams and food plants withered.

"We must go away," the people said. "We must seek a better land." While men made ready the canoes, women brought rolls of mats and *kapa*. What food they had was packed in gourds and, with heavy hearts, the people left their homes.

But two old men refused to go. "We have lived here all our days," they said, "and will not leave. We have prayed for rain, and rain will come. See that hog-shaped cloud."

The others looked, but there was no hope in their faces. "Clouds come," they said, "but no rain falls. Come with us. Here is only death." Still the old men refused. Sadly the others sailed away.

They found a place where rain fell. They built houses and planted gardens, but thought often of the homes that they had left. "If only there were water, life would be better there," they said to one another. "And what of the old men?" they sometimes asked. "We should not have left them. With no water for the gardens they will starve."

"They would not come," others replied.

"But now they will. Lonely and hungry, they will come to us. We must send for them." Young men were

93

chosen. They paddled along the coast and came at last in sight of the village where they used to live.

The old men saw them and came running. "Aloha!" they shouted. "It is good that you have come."

"We came for you," the young men told them as they reached the shore. "Get your things."

"Come with us first," the old men urged. "There is something you must see." Unwillingly the others followed.

The old men led them past the gardens which they had left dry and dead. Now taro stood in water. Sugar cane, sweet potatoes and bananas, all were green and sturdy plants. The young men wondered. They heard the gurgle of a little stream and then the splash of falling water. They followed the old men through a grove of trees and suddenly, not far away, they saw a waterfall. The young men rubbed their eyes and stared. "Where does it come from?" they asked at last.

"It is the good gift of the gods," the old men told them. "After you were gone our prayers were answered. Rain fell, and when it stopped we heard this sound. We found the waterfall. During dry months as well as wet the water flows. We call it Water Without Source."

Wondering still, the young men thanked the gods. "We shall bring back our families," they said. So that place became once more a good home for these people.

Translated by Mary Kawena Pūku'i from a Hawaiian newspaper

THE SUN'S IMPRISONMENT

A wicked chief of Far Kahiki seized the sun and made him prisoner. He put the sun in a great cave and blocked the entrance with huge lava rocks. "Let darkness rule the world!" he shouted and laughed at the evil he had done. "Be ready, my warriors," he warned. "Someone may try to free the sun. I have set a bird watcher at the cave mouth to warn us if he hears a sound. We must be ready to rush out, for we shall keep the sun forever prisoner."

Darkness ruled the earth. The *kapa* would not dry, plants died, and sickness spread because of lack of sunlight and good food. Men shivered as they crept about on cold, dark islands.

On O'ahu a council was called. Men groped their way to the meeting place and tried to make a plan. "What shall we do," they asked, "to rid the world of darkness? Someone must free the sun." Then all were silent. How could they reach Kahiki over the dark ocean? And what of the watchful bird? What of the evil chief with many warriors?

At last Ka'ulu spoke, largest and bravest of all the men. "I will try," he said solemnly. "If I die, I die! But if I should succeed we shall be free of darkness."

"Yes, Ka'ulu," the others said. "You are a huge man and brave. You are the one to go, while we stay here and pray the gods to give you wisdom and great power."

While they prayed Ka'ulu waded bravely through the ocean. The water came to his ankles, then to his knees. On and on that huge man waded and came at last to

96

Far Kahiki. There he saw gleams of light. The sun! His light shone out through tiny openings around the lava rocks.

Following those gleams Ka'ulu stole silently toward the cave. He saw the chief's bird, perched above. With one swift motion he seized the bird and killed it. Then he rolled away the rocks. As the sun crept out, Ka'ulu caught him and threw him up with mighty power to shine once more upon the world.

He waded off, then stopped to shout, "*E*, you evil chief! Where is your prisoner?"

The wicked chief woke at the call and shouted to his warriors. As they rushed from their sleeping house they were dazzled by bright sunlight. They ran to the cave. The bird was dead, and lava rocks rolled down the mountain slope. There rode the sun far, far above them, out of reach.

Since that time the sun shines every day upon our world.

Told by Mary Kawena Pūku'i

"STINGY KAMAKA"

A t Kōke'e, in the mountains of Kaua'i, there is a barren spot where plants will never grow. This is the story of that piece of ground.

It was once the garden of Kamaka. Taro, sweet potatoes, bananas, sugar cane all grew there in abundance. When there was more than Kamaka's family could eat the good food rotted, for Kamaka never shared. If a hungry traveler came by he was met with surly looks and the eating house was closed. "Be off!" Kamaka shouted. "We have only enough for ourselves." "Stingy Kamaka" was well known in the neighborhood.

One afternoon a certain giant, returning to his mountain cave, was lost in mist. He wandered long, stumbling over rocks, tangled by vines and bushes. At last he saw a clearing. He reached it and rejoiced to find a garden full of food plants. "Aloha!" he shouted. "Have you shelter for a tired traveler?"

Kamaka's face appeared in the doorway. "Be off!" he called. "There is nothing here for beggars," and he closed the doorboard. Only tiny gleams of light shone out to tell the shivering stranger of a warm fire within.

The giant lay down at the forest's edge and tried to sleep. But in the night mist turned to heavy rain, and he was drenched and cold.

Daylight came at last and the giant found his way back to his cave home, wet, cold, and very angry.

Next night he came again — to work in Kamaka's garden. When that farmer woke he found every one of his good plants uprooted! Never again did plants grow in that spot for, if he planted, the giant came at night to uproot the plants. And still he comes, to make sure nothing grows on that land which once belonged to "Stingy Kamaka."

Told by Mary Kawena Pūku'i

HOW O‘AHU BECAME ONE ISLAND

A brother and sister lived apart, each on an island. "This is not good," the brother said. "We love each other and, separated, we are lonely. Let us hook our islands together."

"Yes," the sister answered, "I shall hook my small island of Wai‘anae to your larger Ko‘olau island. Our islands shall be one." So they seated themselves and hooked fingers with each other. Closer and closer they pulled their islands till they became one. Then brother and sister lived together on their island of O‘ahu.

Told to Mary Kawena Pūku‘i
by a native of Makua, O‘ahu

THE FLYING TARO

A certain chief of Kona had a taro patch of which he was very proud, and the plants themselves were proud because they grew so tall and green. In an upper corner grew two friends, the tallest and greenest of all those taro plants.

The wind rustled their leaves until the two could whisper to each other. "Listen!" said one, "I hear the sound of chopping. Someone is cutting wood to heat the *imu*."

At that moment a servant came. He stopped near the two plants as if pulling weeds, and whispered to them, "The wood is being chopped and the *imu* is prepared. Soon one will come to pull you two, for I heard the chief order him to take the two large plants that grow here at the upper end." The servant slipped away.

"We are to be pulled!" the two said fearfully, "Pulled, cooked, and pounded into *poi!* No! Let us hide and live!" They hid close to the bank in the shelter of a young banana plant.

They saw a servant come to the upper corner. "The two tall plants," they heard him say. "No two are taller than the others, but all are strong and green. I'll take these two." He pulled some plants and went away.

"We have escaped!" whispered the leaves of the two who hid.

But their escape was not for long. One day the chief walked through his patch. "Why, here are those two plants!" he said. "I thought they grew there in the upper corner." He called a servant. "These two are large," he told him. "Be sure to take them tomorrow to be cooked and pounded into *poi*." Again the two plants fled. This time they hid where long leaves of cane were drooping to the ground. The servant could not find them.

Days passed, then the chief found their hiding place. "So you escaped, you two!" he cried. "You'll not escape again!" This time he marked the place and called a man to come at once to pull the taro.

"We must not wait!"the plants exclaimed. They rose in the air, their leaves serving as wings, and flew to the patch of a common farmer. "Here we are safe," they said. And so it seemed. For days they lived unnoticed.

Then came the servant who had been their friend. "The chief knows you are here." he whispered. "The farmer told him, and he has sent me to pull you up. I go now for my digging stick. Save yourselves." Away they flew, their leaves trembling with fear.

Again and again this happened until one day the chief himself came for them, digging stick in hand. The taro plants rose in air and flew toward the south. The chief saw and followed with an angry shout. People left their work to watch. Some shouted to the chief, "You are close upon them! You will catch them in a moment!" Others prayed that the plants might have power to escape.

Tired out, the two sank down to rest in a friendly field. "Do not stay here!" shouted the plants about them. "The chief is even now hunting in this patch. Fly on! Soon you will reach Kaʻū where he cannot harm you."

The plants arose on tired wings. The chief saw them and gave chase. He was only a step behind! Suddenly he

R. BURNINGHAM

stopped for he had reached the border. His taro plants were in Ka'ū!

"Here!" someone called. "This is the patch of our good chief. Rest here!" The tired plants sank down.

They were, indeed, in the patch of a good chief. Hearing of their escape, he came to look at them. "In this field you are safe," he said. "No man shall harm you. Live in peace."

And so they did. Happy in each other, proud and happy in the young taro plants about them, they lived to a good old age.

This story means that, in the old days, men had the right to leave the land of a cruel chief, and live unharmed in the district of a good one.

From "Legends of Gods and Ghosts" by Westervelt

NAUGHTY 'ELEPAIO

M an was coming down the mountain with a full water gourd. Such a long, hot, rough trail, all the way up to the spring and down again! In the shade of a rock he stopped to rest. A little breeze reached him with cooling fingers. Man sat down, leaned against the cool rock, and fell asleep.

Along came a small, curious *'elepaio* bird. He lighted on a tree to look at Man. Then he flew to the rock and cocked his head this way and that as he made sure Man was asleep. At last he hopped down to the water gourd and examined it with his bright eyes. Back went his head and hammer, hammer, hammer, his small bill struck the gourd until a tiny hole appeared. 'Elepaio watched the water trickle through the hole, then flew back to the tree.

Man awoke and picked up his gourd. How light it felt! Then he noticed a wet spot where the gourd had rested. He saw the hole. "Who has done this?" he asked angrily. He caught sight of 'Elepaio. "Naughty bird!" he shouted and aimed a pebble.

The pebble struck 'Elepaio's leg, and away flew the angry bird. He found 'Io, the hawk. "O friend 'Io," he shouted, "help me! Help me to punish Man!"

"What has Man done?" asked 'Io sharply. "If Man has harmed a little bird, he shall indeed be punished!"

"He threw a stone and hit my leg. See!" and 'Elepaio limped as he hopped along a twig.

"Why did Man do that?" 'Io asked. "What had you done?"

"Nothing at all!" answered 'Elepaio innocently. "I only pecked a little hole in his water gourd."

"And let out all the water that he brought from the mountain spring!" 'Io exclaimed. "I don't blame Man for being angry! Be off, you naughty bird!"

'Elepaio went to Pueo, the owl. "I need your help, Pueo," he said. "I need your help to punish Man. See what he has done to me!"

"Poor little bird!" said Pueo kindly. "What a cruel thing for Man to do! What had you done to him?"

"I didn't even touch him!" 'Elepaio exclaimed. "I only pecked a hole in his water gourd, a tiny hole."

"Oh, naughty 'Elepaio! All the water could run out a tiny hole. I don't blame Man for being angry. Be off with you!"

So 'Elepaio flew away and found 'I'iwi, but 'I'iwi too called him a naughty bird. At last he came to 'Amakihi flitting about among *lehua* blossoms. "O 'Amakihi," he cried, "see what Man has done! See how lame I am all because of that cruel Man!"

'Amakihi hopped about watching the limping bird. "Too bad! Too bad!" he chirped. "What had you done, 'Elepaio? What had you done?"

"Nothing! Nothing but peck a tiny hole in his water gourd!"

"Served you right!" chirped 'Amakihi, hopping about and shaking his tail as if he laughed at 'Elepaio. "Served you right!"

"Useless bird!" shouted 'Elepaio angrily.

"Maybe I'm useless," chirped 'Amakihi, shaking his tail again, "but at least I don't go about making trouble!"

Told by Mary Kawena Pūku'i

106

THE CAVE OF MĀKĀLEI

Mākālei was a small boy when his family went to live in Kona on Hawai'i. Father had always been a farmer and started at once to make a garden. "You cannot farm here," a neighbor said. "You are lucky if you get water to drink. There is none for plants."

Mākālei heard what the neighbor said and he heard his father answer, "If a man prays and works, his garden will grow."

"My father is right," the boy thought. Every day the father made offering to the gods with prayer, every day he worked among his plants.

But no rain fell. The garden was dry. The boy helped his father break up hard lumps of earth so that roots might grow. He learned prayers and prayed earnestly. Still no rain fell, and plants were dying.

Man and boy walked slowly beside their dying plants. "It is no use," the father said. "I should have listened to the neighbors. Here my family will starve."

"Father!" Mākālei stopped suddenly. "There is wind, a cool wind!"

Father walked ahead. "Today there is no wind," he said, "only hot sunshine."

The boy was on his knees searching. "Here, father!" he exclaimed. "Here is a hole, and cool wind comes from it. It comes right out of the ground."

The man turned back and knelt beside his son. "Wind blowing from the ground!" he said. "That is very strange." With a rock he hammered until the hole was larger. "Look down, boy," he directed. "Your eyes are younger than mine. What do you see?"

At first Mākālei saw only darkness. But at last he said, "It is a cave. I can't see clearly, but I hear a dripping sound."

As the boy rose the father brought sticks and grass to cover the hole. "Say nothing of this," he commanded. "Tonight we shall find out the meaning of that dripping sound."

After dark the father pounded until the hole was larger, then lowered Mākālei through it and followed him. A torch of *kukui* nuts showed the two that they were in a cave. It was large enough for Father to stand. In the torchlight the walls of the cave shone wet. Water dripped from the roof. "Do not tell your mother and sisters," father said. "We shall surprise them with good vegetables."

Next day man and boy got logs. When darkness came again they took the logs into the cave. They worked with stone tools, praying as they worked. Before many nights had passed the logs were hollowed like canoes and were catching the dripping water. Each morning Mākālei and his father carried water from their canoes to the thirsty garden. "Won't mother be surprised when she eats sweet potatoes!" the boy thought happily. "What will my sisters think when they have juicy sugar cane to chew!"

But a growing garden is hard to hide. "The gods have blessed us," the mother said.

Neighbors stopped. "Your garden is green and full of food," they told Mākālei with wonder.

"My father prays and works," the boy replied.

At last the secret came out. "Your son is blessed by the gods who showed him hidden water," people said and spoke of the cave as the Cave of Mākālei.

Told by Mary Kawena Pūku'i

THE YOUNG CHIEF'S COMPANIONS

The ruling chief of Maui gave his first-born son to the keeping of a trusted warrior and his wife. Many days passed, and the chief longed for his baby. "I shall go secretly," he told himself, "and see whether my son has the care that a young chief should have."

So the ruler came to the Moloka'i village where that warrior lived. He came alone, paddling a single canoe. He found the warrior's home and, nearby in a shady spot, he saw two little boys. One held a baby, the chief's son, while the other fed the little one. What was the food he was putting, bit by bit, into the child's mouth? Unnoticed, the chief drew closer. Taro tops, cooked taro tops! Was that food fit for a young chief? The father was filled with rage.

"Where are your parents?" he demanded in loud tones.

The little boys glanced up, surprised at the sight of a tall stranger. "Our father is working in the taro patch," said the older boy quietly. "Our mother has gone to the forest for bark to dye her *kapa*."

"And is there no fish," the chief asked, "that you feed that child with taro tops?"

"There is much fish," the boy replied. "But this little one is a young chief and very precious. 'If he cries, feed him,' our father said. 'Feed him cooked taro tops, not fish, lest he choke on a bone and die.'" The boys paid no more attention to the stranger, but continued to feed

111

the baby till he was satisfied and fell asleep. Then the older boy laid him carefully on a mat. The chief watched every movement. He saw that both boys treated the child with great respect. The older held the baby carefully, but never once placed his hand above the head of the little chief. With a grunt of satisfaction the ruler left the children and returned to his canoe.

When their father came, the boys told him they had taken good care of the precious baby. "A man was here," said one, "a tall stranger who came in a canoe. He watched us feed the little chief, then went away."

"Our ruler!" thought the father. Had he been satisfied or angry at what he saw?

Later the chief sent for this warrior. "Let my son return to his home," was his command, "and send your boys to serve him. Your sons shall be attendants and companions of the little chief, for I have watched them. Like you, they can be trusted."

From a Hawaiian newspaper, translated by Mary Kawena Pūku'i

HOW 'UMI FOUND HIS FATHER

"*E! 'Umi!*" The shout rose from a crowd of small boys on the beach, as two surfers came rushing toward land. The taller boy fell with a splash as he neared the last line of breakers, but the smaller one stood until his board reached shallow water. Then he sprang off to wade ashore. His shouting companions joined him, eagerly carrying his surfboard.

"O 'Umi," a friend exclaimed, "you won the race, and Lako is a bigger boy."

"Yes, he's a head taller than you," another added. "But, 'Umi, you have cut your foot on coral. It is bleeding."

"That is nothing," 'Umi replied. "Someday I shall be a warrior. Does a warrior weep over a coral scratch? I am hungry. Let us find food," and he led his companions to his home.

Outside the men's eating house stood a branch firmly set in the ground. From it hung gourds in net containers. 'Umi quickly untied these nets and opened the gourds. "Here is *poi*," he said, offering the food to his friends, "and here is fish and some bananas cooked in the *imu*. Eat all you want. There is much here."

The boys squatted in the shade and ate hungrily. For a time no one spoke. Then, as he scraped the last bit of *poi* from the second gourd, 'Ōma'o said, "We've eaten every bit of food, 'Umi. Won't your father be angry?"

"Perhaps!" 'Umi replied. "What of it? His garden is full of plants."

"But weeding taro is hard work," said 'Ōma'o slowly, "and pounding *poi! Auē!* The *poi* pounder grows heavy! Have you ever done that work, 'Umi? Your father will come home hungry and find no food."

"He will bring fish," 'Umi said carelessly. "We'll make a fire and cook them over coals. I'll do that while father rests. *E!* I can smell those broiled fish now!"

'Ōma'o laughed. "You always have an answer, clever one," he said. He looked about. The other boys, well fed, had wandered off. Suddenly 'Ōma'o threw his arms about his friend. "O 'Umi," he cried, "you are the one I love the most in all the world. I helped to eat your food. Your father will punish you, and I don't want him to. Let him whip me instead."

"You are more than a friend," said 'Umi. "I shall adopt you as my 'son.' Then you can live with me, and we'll share the beatings.

"Now you are my son," he went on, "I'll tell you a secret, 'Ōma'o. My 'father' is only my foster father."

'Ōma'o stared at his companion, then exclaimed, "Is that true, 'Umi? You never said that before."

"Only last night my mother told me."

"Who is your real father?" 'Ōma'o asked.

"I do not know. Just as I asked my mother, someone called. She had no time to answer. I shall ask again when we are by ourselves."

But 'Umi did not need to ask. Next morning the mother said, before them all—foster father and the boys—"'Umi is the chief's son."

The three stared at her, puzzled. "The chief's?" the foster father questioned. "You mean—?"

"Līloa."

"The ruler of Hawai'i? That cannot be." The man spoke wonderingly.

The mother hurried away and returned with a *kapa*-wrapped bundle. From it she took a long feather cloak such was worn by a chief of high rank. She took out also a feather helmet, a chiefly *malo,* and ivory neck ornament. "These are the tokens," she told the three. "Līloa left them for his son, for 'Umi."

They stared in unbelieving silence.

At last 'Umi spoke in a breathless way. "Mother, when shall I go to the chief—my father?"

"The time has come," she answered as she fastened the chiefly ornament about his neck and threw the cloak over his shoulders.

'Ōma'o stared sadly. "You are going away," he said in a small voice.

"And my son is going with me," 'Umi answered confidently. "Tell us of the way, my mother."

"Follow the trail that leads above the sea. The journey will be long, but at last you will reach Waipi'o Valley. From the cliff you can look down upon its fish ponds and taro patches. You will see its sparkling stream and the houses clustered near the base of the cliff. It is a lovely land. You will see the houses of the ruling chief with their *kapu* sticks and guards. Go into the valley, my son, and to the chief's yard. The guardian spirits will recognize you, and you can enter without fear. Sit in your father's lap. He will know the tokens and claim you as his son."

Suddenly 'Umi threw his arms about his mother and held her close. "O Mother," he said, and in his eyes were tears of joy and sorrow. "You and my foster father have cared for me all my life. If the high chief shall, indeed, claim me as his son, I shall care for you." The boy turned to face the trail. "Come, 'Ōma'o," he said. "Let us be on our way."

All day the boys tramped, stopping only twice to rest and eat food the foster father had provided. As they finished the cold broiled fish 'Ōma'o asked, "Where shall we get more food?"

'Umi drew himself up as he replied, "I am a chief. People will give us food."

The boys had journeyed far. The sun was in the western sky, and the trees cast long shadows. Suddenly they heard shouts. "Games!" 'Umi exclaimed. "Let us watch." The two rounded a turn in the trail and looked down onto a level course below. Boys about their own age were rolling *maika* stones. It was fun to watch them, unobserved.

After a time the game ended, and the two saw the boys preparing for a race, on the cliff trail. "They are coming this way," 'Umi whispered, and he and 'Ōma'o drew back into the bushes. They heard a shout to start the racers. Then there were cheers for one ahead. Now panting breath and quick footfalls drew near. 'Umi stepped forward to watch, just as a tall boy darted past, followed by another.

As they passed a certain tree the runners slowed. They stopped, and the second turned to call, "Pi'imai has won!"

"*E! E!* Pi'imai!" came the shout from the crowd hurrying along the trail.

Now Pi'imai, the winner, saw 'Umi. He stared at this boy even smaller than himself, yet wearing feather cloak and helmet. "Are you a chief?" he asked in awe, and his eyes were large with wonder.

"Yes, I am 'Umi."

"Where are you going?" the runner spoke once more. His voice was still hushed in wonder.

"To Waipi'o."

Suddenly Pi'imai fell on his knees. "O heavenly one," he exclaimed, "let me go with you. I long to serve a chief. I will be your loyal follower."

"You shall be my 'son,'" 'Umi replied.

"Oh yes," laughed Pi'imai, "I'm the baby son grown up in one day! Come, heavenly one, to my home for food and rest. Then I shall ask my parents to let me go with you." Pi'imai rose from his knees to show the way.

'Umi was received with honor and kindness. The boys ate and slept. Next morning they were three companions as they took the trail, for Pi'imai's parents had said, "Our son is yours, heavenly one. Let him live in your service."

Once more on their journey, the boys met still another who asked to be 'Umi's follower. This boy was named Ko'i. He too invited the three companions to his home, and his parents also consented to his becoming 'Umi's foster son.

At last the four boys stood on the cliff overlooking Waipi'o Valley. "It is as my mother said," 'Umi whispered, "a land of beauty."

For some time the three "sons" gazed silently on the lovely, narrow valley with steep cliffs rising on either side, a sparkling stream winding among its gardens, and the deep blue of ocean at its foot. But 'Umi's eyes were on a certain group of houses. "There is the home of my father," he was thinking as he saw the crossed sticks at the entrance. Aloud he said, "Let us go down."

No one spoke as the four made their way down the steep trail. All were excited. 'Umi felt himself trembling, and his mouth was dry. Near the chief's home he stopped his companions. "Wait here," he whispered, "while I go on alone. After a time you may hear the sound of drums. That will tell you I am safe, and you will be sent for. If you hear no welcoming sound you will know that I am dead. My father has failed to recognize me. Return quickly to your homes."

'Umi went toward the *kapu* entrance of Līloa's yard. He walked boldly with head held high, but his heart was pounding, and he panted as if from a hard run.

The entrance was barred by sacred crossed sticks. No guard recognized the young chief and removed the sticks, but the guardian spirits knew him, and the sticks fell to let him pass.

Fearlessly, yet tense with excitement, 'Umi entered the house where a chief sat on a platform, resting on fine mats. On either side stood a *kāhili* bearer. This chief was Līloa, ruler of Hawai'i, and—his father. 'Umi sprang forward and into the chief's lap.

Līloa gazed at the boy in amazement. "Whose child are you?" he asked, and his voice was low and gentle as if he already knew the answer.

"Yours! I am 'Umialīloa."

The ruler recognized the tokens which the boy wore, his arms went close about his son, and he wept with joy. After a moment he called a servant. "Let the drums sound," he commanded. "Let them welcome 'Umi."

Then the chief asked, "Had you no traveling companions?"

"I had three. They are my adopted sons."

"Send for them," the father commanded and chuckled softly. To himself he said, "He is only a boy, yet already he has foster sons. Some day he will be father to the people of Hawai'i."

From "Moʻolelo o Hawaiʻi" by S. M. Kamakau, published in a Hawaiian newspaper and translated by Mary Kawena Pūkuʻi

CAN YOU KEEP A SECRET?

Poko was fishing with Grandfather. They had come out at dawn, and the boy had watched the daylight grow. Ocean and sky were pink like a pearl shell, all but one low gray cloud—a low gray cloud that rested on the waves.

They paddled toward the cloud, and it rose slowly, uncovering an island. This island was more green and beautiful than anything the boy had ever seen, and it was filled with growing things. Tall coco palms were heavy with ripe nuts, bananas shone like the sun itself, plants, vines, and trees were large and very green. Suddenly a cock crowed, and the cloud settled down once more upon the island.

"Grandfather!" the boy whispered. "What is that land? Let us go there!"

"It is one of the hidden islands of Kāne, and we cannot go to it."

"Why not, Grandfather? Didn't you see how green and beautiful it is? I want to go there. I want to see it all. Come, Grandfather, let us go."

"Grandson," the old man answered solemnly, "this I have heard: If the gods move that land close to the homes of men, then one can reach it in an hour. But often the land is hidden, and one may sail the ocean until he is gray-headed and never find it. Today the gods gave us sight of that fair land, and then they hid it. It is gone from us forever." The boy said no more, but his heart was filled with longing.

Poko became a man, married, and had a fine family whom he loved. Still the thought of that beautiful green island stayed with him. Still he longed to go there.

Today he and his family were in Puna visiting relatives. His wife and her cousins talked together of *kapa*-making and other women's matters. Tired of listening, Poko wandered off along the beach. He found a shady spot and sat down to rest. He leaned against a rock and dreamily watched a log rolling in the surf. Up the beach it came, pushed by the waves, then down again. As he watched, Poko thought again of the hidden island. If only he might go there! Perhaps he slept.

Suddenly he was roused by a hand upon his shoulder. He sprang up and looked into the face of a woman he had never seen before. Her *pā'ū* was of dark seaweed, her *lei* and bracelets were of shells. "You dream of the hidden island of Kāne," she said, and her voice was like the song of pebbles washed by the waves. "I am the daughter of Kāne. I will take you to that hidden land. Come with me."

The young man followed the stranger down the beach. He saw her touch the rolling log. It became a canoe, and they stepped in. The woman paddled.

The canoe slipped through the waves as swiftly as a fish and as quietly. Poko's heart was full of joy. He did not know whether they paddled a short distance or far when, just ahead, he saw the low-lying cloud. It lifted, and underneath he saw the good green land he had seen long ago.

The canoe scraped on the beach. The two jumped out, carried the canoe up on the sand and looked about them. It was as the young man remembered only more beautiful. Strange trees dropped ripe fruit. Strange

birds sang. Here was a garden where sugar cane reached far above his head. Sweet potatoes burst from the rich earth. Ripe bananas and breadfruit dropped from plant and tree. A fat pig waddled through the garden, so well-fed it only sniffed the fruit. A fat dog lay sleeping in the sun. Farther on, he saw a hen sitting on eggs among the grasses. Another called softly to her chicks. It was a home-like land—only there were no people and no homes.

The young man turned to the woman who still walked at his side. "I want to stay!" he said. "Oh, let me live here always!"

"You may stay," she answered.

Suddenly, with the eyes of his mind, Poko saw his wife. He saw the white flowers about her head, her hand resting lovingly on the fat baby. And he saw his girl and boy. Turning to the daughter of Kāne he said, "I cannot stay alone. I want my wife and children."

"Can you keep a secret?" the woman asked.

The young man looked at her in wonder. "Yes," he answered.

"Then you and your family may live here all your lives."

The two launched the canoe and paddled back to Puna. As they stepped out, their canoe became once more a log rolled by the waves.

The daughter of Kāne spoke earnestly to Poko. "Keep your secret well. Do not tell anyone where you have been. Do not tell anyone where you are going. When six days have passed bring your family to this beach. If you have kept your secret I will come for you, and you shall live upon the hidden island." Then she was gone.

The young man hurried home in great excitement. His wife saw his excitement and his joy. "What has happened?" she asked.

He smiled. "I cannot tell you," he answered. "In six days go with me to the beach, you and the children. Then you shall know."

Others were about. There was talk and laughter, and the wife said no more, but that night when they were alone she asked again. "I cannot tell," he repeated.

"If you love me you must tell," she begged.

He tried to put her off, but still she begged. At last he asked her, "Can you keep a secret?"

She looked at him surprised and answered, "Yes, I can."

Then he told her, "Today I visited the hidden land of Kāne. Six days must pass. Then we can all go there to live—you and the children and I. Only remember: No one must know. We must keep the secret." They talked long that night. He told her of the beauty of that land, of its fruit and vegetables, its pigs and chickens. They were so excited they could hardly sleep.

Next morning the children noticed the excitement and the joy. "What is it, Mother?" they asked. "What is going to happen?"

"I cannot tell," the mother answered. "It is a secret. When six days have passed your father will take us all to the beach over there. Then you will know."

"We want to know now!"

"What is it, Mother? We can keep a secret."

At last she told. "Remember," she whispered, "no one must know."

Six days is a long time to wait. The little daughter whispered to her friend, "Can you keep a secret?" Then she told her that the whole family were going to do what no family had ever done. The daughter of Kāne would take them to a hidden land.

"Can you keep a secret?" the boy asked the friend who surfed with him. "We are going to an island where there is the best surfing in the world," and he too told.

The day came. Before the sun had risen father, mother and children had reached the beach. But they were not alone! The news had spread. Quietly the neighbors gathered. All the village had come to see them off.

There was the log rolling up the beach and down, washed by the waves, but the daughter of Kāne did not come. The log did not change to a canoe. Poko looked longingly over the ocean. "I did not keep the secret," he said sadly.

His wife picked up her baby and looked about happily at her friends. "I think we should have been very lonely in that hidden land," she whispered.

Told to Mary Kawena Pūku'i by an old man
whose mother came from Puna

124

INDEX

INDEX

The 'Ahahui 'Ōlelo Hawai'i, the association of Hawaiian language teachers, recommended a uniform spelling system in 1978. Among their suggestions, which are observed in this book, is one to delete the dashes or hyphens that have been used to separate the syllables in proper names and common nouns. They urge the use of the *'okina* (glottal stop [']), and the *kahakō* (macron [ˉ]) in writing all words which should have these diacritical marks. In addition, the singular and plural of Hawaiian nouns are the same, with the plural being indicated in Hawaiian speech by the use of an article such as *nā* or *mau* before the noun, rather than by adding "s."

Pronunciation of vowels:

a as in f*a*ther

e as *ay* in m*ay*

  or as *e* in m*e*n

i as *ee* in *see*

  or a shorter, quicker *ee*

o as in m*o*re

u as *oo* in f*oo*d

aku: A large fish, a kind of ocean bonito, 46, 47

'*alae*: Mud hen, 27, 28, 29, 30, 31, 32

aloha: A common greeting, 37, 46, 50, 53, 55, 59, 76, 78, 90, 94, 98

'*amakihi*: A small bird whose yellow feathers were used for capes and helmets, 106

auē: Alas, 15, 57, 114

'*awa*: A drink made from the '*awa* shrub, 47, 52, 55, 60, 62, 63

e: A call for attention, 57, 90, 97, 113, 114, 116

'*elepaio*: A bird, a flycatcher, 105–107

'Ewa: A district, O'ahu, 48, 50, 52

126

INDEX

Hāʻena: Caves near northern shore of Kauaʻi, 11
hala: A tree, 80, 81, 82, 83
Haleakalā: Volcano, Maui, 20, 38, 44
Hanakahi: A fisherman of ʻEwa, 53, 54
Haʻo: A chief and chiefess of Oʻahu, 86, 87, 88, 89
hau: A tree whose light-weight wood was used for outriggers, etc.,
    and whose bark was used for cordage, 31
Hawaiʻi: An island; name of the island group, 18, 25, 32, 37, 38, 44,
    46, 47, 52, 108, 114, 118
heiau: A place of worship, 55
Hiʻiaka: Youngest sister of Pele, 66
Hilo: A district, Hawaiʻi; village of that district, 19, 38, 78
Hina: Woman's common name; mother of Māui, 21, 34, 35, 36,
    37, 38
Hōlua Manu: The Slide of the Bird, 71
Hualālai: Volcano, Hawaiʻi, 12
hula: A dance with rhythm accompaniment, 44

ieʻie: A vine whose roots were used for basket making, etc., 34
ʻiʻiwi: A small bird, 106
imu: A ground oven in which food is cooked by means of hot stones,
    8, 15, 32, 47, 74, 76, 81, 113
ʻio: A large hawk, 105

ka: The, 82
Kahiki: Tahiti; Far Kahiki was a term for any land beyond the place
    "where the sky rests upon the sea" around the Hawaiian Islands,
    43, 46, 55, 96, 97
Kāhili: A feather standard; symbol of a chief, 118
kahuna: One wise in some kind of work; sometimes a priest, 55,
    58, 68
Kamaka: A man of Kōkeʻe, Kauaʻi; 98–99
Kamōʻiliʻili: A region, Oʻahu, included in the present city
    of Honolulu, 80
Kanaloa: One of the great gods, 52, 53, 55, 56, 58
Kāne: One of the great gods, 15, 52, 53, 55, 56, 58, 119, 120, 122,
    123, 124
kapa: Bark cloth; the Tahitian form, tapa, is in common use, 7, 9, 20,
    21, 28, 35, 67, 84, 88, 93, 96, 111, 115, 120

kapu: Sacred, forbidden, 88, 89, 118
Ka'ū: A district, Hawai'i, 102, 104
Kaua'i: An island, 43, 46, 47
Ka'ulu: A strong man, or giant, of O'ahu, 96, 97
Kawaiaha'o: The-waters-of-Ha'o, spring within the present city of Honolulu. This spring no longer flows, 89
Kawena: Mrs. Pūku'i's name, 59, 63
Kealoha: A woman of O'ahu, 80, 81, 82
Keoha: A canoe-maker of Hilo, 78–79
Kewalo: Spring and land section, O'ahu, within present city of Honolulu, 84
Kila: Son of Mo'ikeha, ruling chief of Kaua'i, 46, 47
Kīlauea: Volcano, Hawai'i, 44
koa: A tree, 3, 6
Kohala: A district, Hawai'i, 74
Ko'i: Companion and "son" of 'Umi, 117
Kōke'e: A mountain region, Kaua'i, 98
Kona: A district, Hawai'i; the lee side, 101
Ko'olau: A range of mountains, O'ahu, 100
Ko'olau Loa: Long Ko'olau; a district, O'ahu, 90
Kou: Village at mouth of Nu'uanu Stream, O'ahu, 51, 87
Kū'ili: A hill on the slope of Hualālai, 12–15
kukui: A tree whose nuts are used for oil, 64, 65, 109
Kuna Mo'o: A giant lizard of Hawai'i, 37, 38, 39
Kū'ula: God of fishing, 27

Lā'ie: A land section and village, windward O'ahu, 48, 50, 51
Laka: A man of Kaua'i; also the goddess of *hula*, 3–6
Lē'ahi: Crater, O'ahu; now called Diamond Head, 43
lehua: Blossoms from the *'ōhi'a* tree, 106
lehua lei: A garland of flowers from the *'ōhi'a* tree, 44
lei: A garland of flowers, 57, 120
Līloa: A ruling chief, Island of Hawai'i, 118

maika: A game; also stone used in the game, 116
Mākālei: A boy of Kona, Hawai'i, 108–110
Makiki: A land section, O'ahu, in present city of Honolulu, 86
Makua: A farmer of windward O'ahu, 55–58
malo: Man's loin cloth, 7, 57, 115

INDEX

mānele: A litter for carrying a person, 88
Mānoa: Valley, O'ahu, 80
manu: Bird, 70–71
Maui: An island, 18, 43, 44, 111
Māui: A hero of Polynesia, 18–40
Mauna Loa: Long-mountain; volcano, Hawai'i, 44
menehune: Little people living in mountain and forest, 4, 6, 8, 9, 10–11, 12, 14, 15
Mo'ikeha: A ruling chief of Kaua'i, 46, 47
Moloka'i: An island, 43, 111
mo'o: Lizard; a giant lizard, 37, 38, 39, 67, 68, 69
mū: A banana-eating tribe of menehune, v
Mūkākā: A man of the Punahou region, O'ahu, 80, 81, 82

Nāmaka: Sister of Pele and goddess of the sea, 43, 44
nei: This, 32, 93
nenue: A species of fish belonging to the pickerel, 59, 60, 63
Nu'uanu: A stream and valley, O'ahu, 51, 87

O'ahu: An island, 18, 43, 48, 52, 72, 80, 90, 93, 96, 100
'ōhi'a: A tree which bears the *'ōhi'a lehua* flower, 14, 15
Ola: A district chief of Kaua'i, 7, 9
'Oma'o: Companion and "son" of 'Umi, 113, 114, 115, 116
'ōpelu: Mackerel, 46, 47

pā'ū: Woman's skirt, 7, 66, 120
Pe'ape'a: Chief of an island of Far Kahiki, 34, 35, 36
Pele: Goddess of the volcano, 43–44, 66
Pī: A man of Kaua'i, 7–9
Pi'imai: Companion and "son" of 'Umi, 116, 117
poi: Food made from *taro*, 6, 8, 9, 46, 53, 55, 101, 102, 113, 114
Poko: A person's name, 119–124
pueo: Owl, 106
Pūku'i: A person's name; literally hub, 59, 63
Puna: A district, Hawai'i, 78, 79, 120, 122
Punahou: A land section, O'ahu, within present city of Honolulu; new-spring, 82

129

Puʻuloa: Pearl Harbor, 52, 54
Puʻuopele: Hill-of-Pele, a hill on Kauaʻi, 43

Rocky Hill: A place in Mānoa Valley, 80

Salt Lake: A fire pit dug by Pele, 43

taro: The vegetable from which *poi* is made. This spelling is more
    commonly used than *kalo*, 6, 8, 31, 50, 94, 98, 101–104, 111
ti: A shrub whose long leaves are used to wrap food, 30, 34, 70, 71

ʻUmi: Son of Līloa, 113, 114, 115, 116, 118

Waiʻanae: Mountains and district, Oʻahu, 72, 100
Waikīkī: Spurting water; a land section, Oʻahu, 48, 51, 81
Wailuku: A river on Hawaiʻi, 37, 40
Waimea: A river, canyon, and district, Kauaʻi, 7, 9, 69, 71
Waipiʻo: A valley, northern Hawaiʻi, 19, 115, 116, 117